Room 202 Animal Quartet
By Susan Clymer

There's a Hamster in My Lunchbox
There's a Tarantula in My Homework
There's a Frog in My Sleeping Bag
There's a Rabbit in My Backpack

Keep an eye out for these other books by Susan Clymer:

Nine Lives of AdventureCat
AdventureCat Goes to School
Four Month Friend
The One and Only Bunbun
The Mermaid Ornament
Halloween Echoes
Scrawny, the Classroom Duck
Llama Pajamas

Runner

Reads
Braille

By Susan Clymer
Cover Art by Micaya Clymer

Dancing Tale Books

ISBN 978-0-557-04017-9

For the Risk Takers...
All of us
Who want to try new feats,
Face our fears,
Run new races.

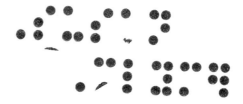

Keep Reading!
Susan Clymer

Contents

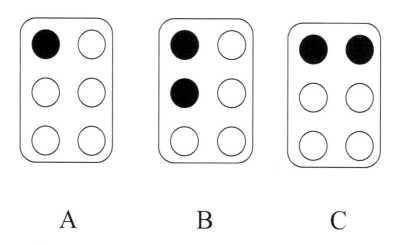

A   B   C

Did you ever want to understand how a blind or visually impaired person reads? Here are the first three letters in the alphabet in Braille.

1
Whistling Boy

Jake zipped past Mom's bedroom and turned a hard right, nabbing a lemon drop from the candy bowl on the table. Still going a hundred miles an hour, he felt for the doorknob. Cold air tingled his nose as he strode outside.

Sure enough, Mom was waiting for him in the car, singing, "I'm as corny as Kansas in August."

Jake found the edge of the porch with his cane, then stepped down. He veered along the brick path and leaped into the back seat of the van. "Let's go!"

Every Saturday, he couldn't wait to meet up with his friends. This was the first year he had been old enough to join the big kids at Adventure Sports. They had ridden bikes in the fall and gone sledding in January.

And he was the newcomer.

The youngest of all.

Popping the sour lemon drop into his mouth, Jake clicked his seat belt. Most of the group's activities happened outside, but this month they were rollerblading at an indoor rink. He pounded out a rhythm of galloping horses on the seatback in front of him as Mom headed down their street. She swerved left onto the big road and picked up speed. Soon, the car slowed. The whir of the engine stopped.

Mom walked him inside the rink, amidst the smell of hot chocolate and the *ping-pong-sproing* of the pinball machines. "See you in three hours," Mom said and left him in the middle of the group.

"Hand-check!" Katherine called.

Everyone joined hands in laughing confusion. It didn't matter whether it was snowing or as hot as a summer day in the desert, Katherine started each meeting with a circle. Today, she asked them to share their favorite flavor of ice cream that began with the same letter as their name.

"Shaniqua's my name, and strawberry ice cream is as sweet as sugar," Shaniqua announced. She was the oldest, in eighth grade. Shaniqua had had cancer as a baby and now wore eyes made out of plastic. *Prostheses,* they were called.

"Brandon, here. I like blueberry cheesecake ice cream." Brandon had been born with sight, but had gone blind four years ago when he was seven.

Feet shuffled. No one spoke.

"Who's next?" Katherine encouraged.

"My name is Eva," Eva said shyly. "And I like *every* kind of ice cream." She wore thick glasses that she had let Jake feel when they sat next to each other on the sledding trip. She'd also given him a slice of the tastiest cheese tortilla he'd ever eaten.

Well, Jake was stuck. The only flavor he could think of that started with a J didn't exist. When it was his turn, he said, "My name's Jake, and someday I'm going to invent *jellybean* ice cream. Maybe on my tenth birthday!"

"Skating time!" Katherine announced, clapping her hands. She had been born blind, like Jake, but she wasn't a child anymore or even a teenager.

Every kid skated with a sighted partner. Swinging the tip of his cane from side to side, Jake found his way down the steps to a bench. His heart pounded faster. Today was *his* turn to try skating all by himself. Katherine had promised.

Jake folded his cane and set it under the bench beside his shoes. A month ago, he had wrapped his hands around his partner's arm and clung like an octopus, his feet rolling out from under him. This afternoon, he stepped onto the rink.

Alone.

At first, he skated with his right hand brushing the wall. Balancing wasn't easy without someone beside him. He pushed off into space. Jake whistled while he skated. He listened for the echo, so he could tell if he was about to bump into a wall.

He listened for the spinning sounds of other kid's skates, too. And their voices. Jake sailed around and around. He liked the smell of the popcorn from the snack bar. He loved the feeling of freedom.

When his legs grew tired, he headed toward a corner. The closer he skated to the corner, the louder the echo of his whistle became. Jake stopped rolling. He dug into his pocket and pulled out a handful of coins. The nickel wasn't the biggest, but it was the thickest. He dropped the nickel and listened. Just as he'd thought, the sound of the coin landing on the hard, polished floor of the skating rink was different than on his bedroom floor at home. He tried a dime.

Soon he heard the rolling whir of rollerblades. *Three sets of rollerblades*, he believed. As Jake swung his hand in an arc across the floor, he heard a girl say, "He's dropping coins on the ground and scrambling around to find them."

It took Jake a few seconds, flipping through the memory file of voices in his head, to realize that it must be Meredith. She was Brandon's cousin, a sighted volunteer who had just started coming on Saturdays. *A teenager.* Jake stood up on his wobbly wheels and dusted off his knees. He was *not* scrambling around.

"What's up?" Brandon said in a gravelly, cool-guy voice. He always smelled like the outdoors to Jake, maybe because he lived with five frogs.

"Drop a coin for me?" Jake asked. "You choose which one."

"Sure," Brandon growled, taking all of Jake's money.

Jake listened as hard as he could. He recognized the clank as a coin landed near his feet. "A nickel," he announced.

"How did you know *that*?" Meredith asked, her voice shooting up.

Pleased, Jake danced in place, but then the toes of his skates swayed outward. *Whoa*, he thought, catching his balance.

"Let me drop one, por favor," Eva begged in her high-pitched voice that came from the height of his shoulder. She was the only kid smaller than he, though she was a year older. Jake had been around Eva long enough to know that *por favor* meant please. "Listen up," she warned.

This time the sound was a jingle.

"A dime?" Jake guessed, noticing that he couldn't hear anyone roller-skating on the rink. Maybe the others were taking a popcorn break.

"Nope, a penny," Eva replied.

"I'm practicing," Jake explained shyly. "Trying to learn a new trick for school." What he really wanted to do was to impress the older kids here at Adventure Sports. He wanted Brandon and Eva and Shaniqua to think of him as a friend, just like he thought of them. But he wouldn't admit that. Not in a million years.

"Here's your penny, Jake," Eva piped.

He felt in the air until he found her hand.

"Let's go, Meredith!" Brandon cried softly. With thump-thump and then a whoosh, the two cousins started skating away.

For a moment, Jake stood frozen. Brandon was stealing his coins?! He ran on his skates for a few steps and then glided after the other boy. His ankles wobbled as he picked up speed. He skated all the way around the oval, following Brandon's triumphant laugh.

Luckily, they had the rink to themselves. "Give me back my money!" Jake cried. He'd never chased anybody on rollerblades before. He imagined one of those ancient trumpets blowing a charge. *Ta Da, ta-ta-ta DA.*

Next, he imagined himself galloping on horseback, wearing armor and carrying a shield with a fire-breathing dragon on the front. Faster and faster, he skated. "Stop, thief," he hollered.

"Never!" Brandon yelled. Their voices echoed, bouncing off the high ceiling. Jake remembered to whistle so he wouldn't crash into a wall.

"Take it easy, boys," Katherine called.

Jake always obeyed Katherine. She was *The Boss*, after all. Right now he was too busy pretending to be a knight galloping off to save the world. Brandon had stopped talking. *The sneak.* It would be harder to catch him if he didn't make noise.

"Brandon," Meredith insisted from across the rink. "Hadn't we better stop?"

Now he was going to nab the thief. "Hah!" Jake shouted, pretending to lift his shield as he sped straight toward Meredith's voice. Just then, he heard the rolling whir of rollerblades. *Too close.* Had the others come back on the rink? He gasped and tried to change direction.

Someone bigger crashed into his shoulder.

"Heellp," Shaniqua groaned, her voice loud and then soft, and then loud again, as if she were spinning in a circle. Jake's knees wobbled in and out. He teetered backward, then forward, then back again. He came to a scrambling stop, still standing.

"Oh my," murmured Mr. Solomon, who was skating with Shaniqua. "Is anyone hurt?"

"I'm fine," Jake panted, but his heart was thumping around in his chest like a panicked frog. He'd almost *crashed* onto that hard floor.

"Well, now, I don't know about me," Shaniqua drawled. "You scared me half to death, boy." She poked him. "Aren't you afraid of anything, Whistling Boy?"

"Whistling Boy?" Jake said. Suddenly, he stood a little taller. Shaniqua seemed to think he was brave. And she was the oldest of them all.

He heard the squeal of stopping rollerblades. "Here's your money," Brandon muttered.

Jake stuffed the change into his pocket. "Guess I'm not a scared sort of guy," he bragged to Shaniqua. And it was the truth.

At least at that very moment...

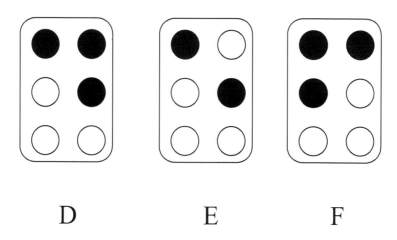

D   E   F

In Braille, the small circles stick up so that you can feel them with your fingers. A visually impaired child starts learning to read letters in preschool.

2
Bert and Wagger

Monday morning, Jake ran his fingers over the first problem in his math workbook. Since he was the only visually impaired student in Ellington Elementary, he had his very own Braille math book. Jake read the dots with his right hand and moved his left hand down the page to make sure he didn't get lost. He was a good Braille reader. In fact, Dad said he could read like a champ.

Jake's parents had divorced when he was two, so long ago he didn't remember. Mom said they were fond of each other, but they hadn't mixed together too well. His father made hippy moccasins and traveled around to sell them at fairs, while Mom was a teacher who liked people and things to stay put. Every week, Dad called to talk to Jake, and he always asked about his friends and his reading.

Jake sighed. He'd *much* rather be reading.

Too bad his Braille copy of *The Lion, the Witch, and the Wardrobe* was too bulky to carry to school.

Arithmetic was harder than eating neatly when he couldn't see the food on his plate. Oh, he understood multiplication. But this problem, fifty-nine divided by seven, seemed *impossible*. The teacher had given him a handful of little blocks she called manipulatives to help.

Jake swung his legs. He drummed his fingers.

For as long as he could remember, he'd made up stories when he was bored. Last year his teacher, Miss Tarantino, hadn't been able to tell whether he was paying attention or daydreaming. It was a great advantage to being blind.

A comforting feeling slipped over Jake as he began to create a story. *The main character could be a blind boy. And his name would be -- Bert. Bert would have a guide dog called...*

Jake imagined the dog, a furry fellow with a long, soft tail.

Why, the guide dog could be named Wagger! Bert would be sixteen, the youngest he could be and have a guide dog. The story would begin on Wagger's second birthday. Bert would make him a cake of dog biscuits.

Jake wiggled his toes as he created. This was getting good.

As Bert walked his dog down the street after the party, he'd hear a strange flapping. Of course, he'd reach down with one hand to check what was making the sound. That's when he would discover that Wagger had grown tiny wings on his feet.

Jake clutched his cane in his lap, laughing silently. Wouldn't it be great if guide dogs could grow wings on their second birthday?

With a WOOF, Wagger fluttered his wings and drifted up into the air.

"Look at that!" a strange woman cried. The mailwoman, probably.

Jake was beginning to feel as he really were Bert, standing on the street corner with his guide dog.

He gripped Wagger's harness. Suddenly, he started rising up, too. He waved at the mailwoman.

"Jake?" a voice said.

"Isn't it amazing?" he hollered to the mailwoman beneath him. "Meet Wagger, my flying guide dog!"

A hand shook his shoulder. "Jake," Ms. Rose insisted firmly.

Jake turned toward the voice. It was his *teacher.* That's when Jake realized that he'd yelled in the middle of math. Not only that, his entire class was laughing. His face blushed as hot as a frying pan.

"Tell me about the flying guide dog," Emily pleaded. She sat beside him. They'd had the same teacher since kindergarten. Often, they sat together at lunch, too, trading cookies and pickles and other good stuff.

"Yeah," sneered Desmond behind him. "Tell us." Only he didn't sound so friendly.

Jake put his head down on his desk and buried his face in his arms. He felt as foolish as he had during his first week in the fourth grade when he'd walked into a closet instead of the boy's bathroom.

"Settle down, class," Ms. Rose ordered. The teacher spoke close to his ear, "I know you can do long division...if you concentrate, Jake." She wore a perfume that smelled like roses. "I'll help you if you get stuck."

When Jake's ears stopped burning, he did try. But he was thirsty. Maybe Ms. Rose would let him get a drink. He started to lift his hand in the air, but then decided against it. No chance she would let him go.

Beside him, he could hear Emily's pencil scribbling. It didn't help to know that most of his classmates could work this problem.

Jake pulled his Braillewriter closer and typed in $59 \div 7$. The Brailler clinked and clanked as it typed the dots on his piece of paper. He checked the dots with his fingers. Wasn't there some trick his vision teacher had taught him about how to line the problem up? Then Jake remembered the manipulatives. Maybe he could divide fifty-nine blocks into groups of seven.

Carefully, Jake counted the blocks into neat stacks around the Brailler. Each tower had seven blocks, and he built eight towers. That made sense. Seven times eight equaled fifty-six.

His mouth suddenly felt as dry as a desert wind. What was he supposed to do with these three extra blocks? And where in the world was he supposed to put that 8 on his paper in the Braillewriter? With a sigh, Jake raised his hand. Was school really supposed to be this hard?

Surely not.

3
Six Steps, Turn

J ake reached for a cereal box in the cupboard to the left of the sink. His mother labeled the top right corner of his snacks in Braille with sticky tape. Hopefully, she hadn't eaten up his favorite. Each day when Mom came home from teaching sixth grade at Thurston Downs, a private school across town, she munched. *Cheerios*, Jake read with his fingers and shook the box. It rattled.

Mom sat at the table, flipping through the mail. As usual, she was singing, "I'm gonna wash that man right out of my hair."

Mom adored old musicals. In college, she'd studied to be a professional singer until she had decided that the world needed more teachers. Now she sang just for fun in a choir called *Sing It Again*. They performed all over town, at concerts and baseball games and even birthday parties.

Every Tuesday, while Mom practiced, he went swimming with Jared and Jeremy and John. The boys played Marco Polo and swam until they turned into prunes. He'd known the "J" brothers his whole life. Their mothers had been best friends in college. Jared was eleven, Jeremy was nine, and John was only four. The two families camped together in the summer, too.

Jake grabbed a bowl from the top shelf and a spoon from the drawer. His stomach growled. Today had been a good day at school. Ms. Rose had let him read the part of the scarecrow in *The Wizard of Oz* from their weekly magazine. The magazine sent him his very own Braille copy. Jake tucked the cereal box under his elbow.

Another envelope ripped. Mom's singing stopped. "Your Adventure Sports Newsletter arrived."

With his free hand, Jake cradled the milk against his chest as he walked across the kitchen. Katherine always sent two copies of the newsletter, one in print and one in Braille. "What are we doing next?" he asked, carefully setting his bowl down on the table.

"Stagecoach Run," Mom said. "It follows the old stagecoach route through town. Goodness, the race is over three miles long!"

Jake almost dropped the milk. "Run?"

From the first Saturday when he'd ridden on a tandem bicycle, he had loved Adventure Sports. It had been the feeling of the wind ruffling his hair. Sailing down a hill on a sled had been out of this world. And horseback riding. In fact, he'd looked forward to each new adventure.

So far.

Jake sat down in his chair with a thump.

Mom kept right on talking, "Practices for the first month will be held at the track at the School for the Blind. In April, the group starts running on a trail."

"What happens," Jake asked, tugging open the cereal box, "if I fall?"

"Listen to this!" Mom exclaimed. "Any money raised goes to Branstock." That was the Kindergarten for visually impaired children he'd attended. Then she added, "You fall all the time sledding."

"Snow is soft," Jake replied, pouring his milk. He dangled one finger over the edge of the bowl so he could feel when the milk covered his cereal.

"Do you fall when you skate?" Mom asked.

"Not much." He skimmed his hand across the table, patting softly with his fingertips to find his spoon. He remembered his near miss last weekend and shivered. "Besides, skating rinks are flat. No gravel."

"Hmm," his mother said. "I guess you could skin your knee."

"Or bash my elbow on a rock!" He *hated* falling outside. It was that moment that seemed to last forever. That frozen instant of sailing through the air, when he had no idea where he might land. What if he ripped every inch of skin off his hands or hit his head?

Three miles of possible falling, he thought. His heart had started hopping inside his chest like a frog again. "Nothing doing," he spluttered.

"I'm gonna' wash that man right out of my hair,"

Mom sang softly, "and send him on his way."

Jake thumped his spoon on the table. "I'm not running!"

"Not running?" Mom repeated.

Now she was paying attention. Jake didn't say another word. He crunched up an entire bowl of the best cereal in the universe, yet he didn't taste a single bite.

Mom didn't sing again either.

Half an hour later, Jake paced back and forth in this bedroom. Oh, he'd tried to read, but he'd just kept running his fingers over the same paragraph again and again, not remembering a single thing he read.

Jake spun an about-face at his door. What was he going to do? If he didn't run in the Stagecoach Run, he wouldn't see Brandon or Eva or Shaniqua for ages.

Two months!

Adventure Sports was his favorite activity. It was even more fun than being the fourth honorary "J" brother every Tuesday night.

Six steps, turn.

Jake tapped his bedpost and reversed direction.

Six steps, turn.

He bit down on his lower lip. This was ridiculous. He was acting as if he'd bumped into a monster. Jake stumbled to a stop halfway to his bed. Actually, that was *exactly* how he felt – as if he'd come nose to nose with the monster that had lived in his closet when he was four years old. The Snoring Monster.

Only this time it was a *running monster*. A creature with a roar that could make his stomach quiver like jelly. A monster in tennis shoes that tripped kids and scared them out of their minds.

Jake started pacing again. He hadn't believed in monsters in *years*. Maybe his mother was right. He was letting his imagination get the better of him.

Spinning on his heel, Jake marched back. For the first four practices, they would meet at the track at the School for the Blind. *Tracks are flat,* Jake thought. *Flat like one of my CD's. Smooth like chocolate icing on a cupcake.*

Grabbing the corner post on his bed, Jake swung himself up into the air. At the right moment, he let go of the bedpost and spun around in a circle. As usual, he landed sitting on his bed.

It had taken him *ages* to perfect that trick. First, he taught himself how to do a running leap onto his bed, hollering, "Beware Flying Boy!" That's what he and the "J" Brothers yelled as they did a cannonball into the pool. Next, Jake had started slapping the high bedpost as he jumped. Finally, he'd grabbed the post and started to soar, spinning, through the air.

Bounce, bounce, bounce.

He would try running. As long as they were practicing on the track he would join his friends.

Bounce, bounce, bounce.

At least for the first month...

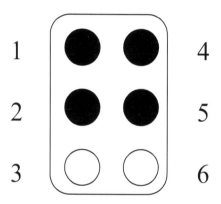

This is called a Braille cell. See how every dot is numbered? This is the letter G. Dots #1, 2, 4, and 5 form the letter G.

4
A Yo-Yo

Wind whipped through Jake's sweatpants as he hopped from foot to foot on the track at the School for the Blind. It was as cold as a popsicle. *No*, as cold as Antarctica. The Boss had asked them to share what experience they'd had running – and the circle was *gigantic*. Something heavy leaned on Jake's leg, and he stopped hopping. At least, it made him warmer. Next, he heard panting.

Why, Socks must be sitting on his toes!

Katherine had told them that her guide dog lived up to his name. He picked up her socks and carried them all over the house. *Dirty socks. Clean socks. Fluffy socks.* Socks loved them all.

For as long as he could remember, Jake had yearned to have a dog bigger than he was. He'd begged for a Great Dane or a Saint Bernard. Mom said he was too young to take care of a pet.

And he had to be at least sixteen before he could get a guide dog. So, he had to wait *forever* – six years and two months. As if the dog understood, Jake felt a soft lick on his fingers. Jake ached to pet him, but the big boy was wearing his harness. That meant he was working, off limits for strokes.

Socks spent his days watching out for cars, unexpected stairs, and trashcans in the middle of nowhere. Ever since the Boss had graduated from college, she'd lived in an apartment, taking buses to work, going out to dinner with friends. Socks guided her every step of the way. Reluctantly, Jake pulled his fingers away.

"Let's run, before we freeze." Katherine clapped her hands. "Ten times around the track today. Eva, you're with Mr. Solomon, like last year." She added in her best general's voice, "Jake, why don't you run with Meredith?" It was not a question.

Oh no! Not Meredith, Jake moaned in his mind. Teenage girls made less sense to him than math.

Silently, Jake took the rope Katherine passed, studying it with his hands. It was a short, soft piece of rope, about a foot and a half long with a knot near each end. With his left hand, Jake grasped one of the knots. This rope wasn't strong enough to hold up a hamster, let alone a boy.

"Ready, Jake?" Meredith asked. He could feel tension on the rope as she picked up her end. Now they would stay together.

Jake lifted his feet and blasted forward. In less than five steps, he knocked into Meredith's side with his shoulder. Quickly, he hopped to the right so he wouldn't step on her foot. The rope jerked him back, and he crashed into her a second time.

"Hey!" Meredith exclaimed.

Great, he'd turned into a human yo-yo. Maybe if he didn't swing his arms so hard. By the first turn, Jake's lungs hurt. He was supposed to jog ten times around this track?

Impossible!

Runners pounded up from behind. "Look out, here comes the Two Dude Express!" Brandon hollered. "We're galloping!" He was running with Adam, the new high school volunteer. Everybody knew Brandon wanted his own horse. He already had five frogs, a snake, and a dog that slept on his feet.

"Stop showing off, Little Cousin," Meredith yelled as the boys zoomed past.

Little Cousin? Jake thought. He'd always considered Brandon big.

"Bet I finish my ten laps first, *Dragon Breath*," Brandon called.

Meredith squeaked indignantly.

"Beep, beep," The Boss sang out like a car horn. She padded past them with her guide dog.

On the other side of the track, Jake heard Shaniqua's lilting voice telling her partner that when she was little she had believed that if she tied a hundred balloons together she'd float up to the stars.

How could everybody be having a good time? Jake trotted along, his lungs burning like fire. Soon he'd be crawling around the loop on his hands and knees. Or he'd be dragging himself by his elbows!

Something little scrambled across the track in front of his feet. Jake stumbled to a stop so quickly he yanked the rope clean out of Meredith's hand. Claws skittered. Socks howled in an *I-want-to-chase* bark.

A chaos of sounds erupted. Big paws scuffled. WOOFS filled the air. "A cat ran under Sock's nose!" Meredith screeched in his ear.

The back of Jake's neck prickled as he listened to stumbling feet and furious muttering. "Leave it!" Katherine commanded, and the scuffling stopped.

Ragged panting continued.

"Anyone would think you'd never seen a cat, Socks," Katherine hissed. Her voice came from halfway up the slope to the school buildings.

Jake groaned. Guide dogs weren't supposed to chase *anything*. And they certainly weren't allowed to drag their owners up a hill. Socks would be in BIG trouble. The tension on his rope pulled him in again.

"Looks like the cat *vanished* into a basement of one of those brick buildings at the top of the hill," Meredith said, as they picked up speed to a fast walk. "The kitty has a chunk missing from one ear."

"You suppose el gato hangs out *here*?" Eva asked, hurrying up behind them with Mr. Solomon.

Gato means cat, Jake guessed. The four of them strolled around the track, side by side. Jake figured this school must be crawling with teachers' guide dogs during the week. "The cat that lived at the School for the Blind," he murmured.

"Good song title," Eva said.

"You like to sing?" Jake already knew she played the keyboard. Eva was homeschooled. On a sledding trip, she'd told him that she was in the fifth grade, mostly. Jake pulled his free hand inside his sweatshirt to warm up his icy fingers. It felt good not to be running. Besides, he was getting the hang of walking with this rope.

"I like to make up songs about my cat," Eva replied. " I've written nine songs about Velvet."

"Nine songs about one cat?" Jake added a hop to his step. If he created a song about a cat, Eva might play it on her keyboard. The two of them could even sing it as a duet for the next Adventure Sports Award Banquet. They'd practice at Eva's house for hours, nibbling on those tasty cheesy tortillas.

Luckily, he was used to daydreaming. A song shouldn't be too hard. First, he needed a tune. The rhythm of his walk helped. Half a lap later, Jake sang to the tune of *Row, Row, Row Your Boat*,

> "Matt, Matt, Matt the cat
> He was very fat,"

"Not like that," Eva interrupted. "Serious songs." She made an odd sniffling sound, poking him. "Fool."

Jake drew his eyebrows together. Eva was usually as quiet as falling snow. Now, he could swear she was muffling a giggle.

"Like in a royal court," Eva added.

A jester, Jake thought. That kind of a fool wasn't bad at all. Jesters sang songs to kings and told jokes. They even played tricks. Jake wondered what he could call Eva. *Shrimp?*

Before he could make up his mind, Eva sang,
        "Matt, Matt, Matt the cat,"
Why, she was finishing his song! Eva had a soft voice, perfectly on pitch. "His best friend was a..."

"Bat," Meredith caroled, not anywhere near the right note.

Jake kept on singing as he marched, changing the words for the second verse,
        "Matt, Matt, Matt the cat
        Always wore a hat."
To his glee, Eva joined in,
        "Matt, Matt, Matt the cat
        His amigo was a..."
Jake had planned to say rat, but Eva sang out, "Wombat."

Jake swung his free arm, as if he were leading a parade in the king's court. *Was a wombat a real animal? Or a make believe one, like a fire-breathing dragon?*

Meredith warbled along with them, completely out of tune. On the other side of the track, Shaniqua and her partner experimented with a low harmony.

In the third verse, the fat cat slept on a mat and his friend turned out to be a gnat. That was The Boss' idea. She didn't sound furious anymore. She must have forgiven Socks.

Another great Saturday at Adventure Sports, Jake thought as he strode around the last two laps, his free arm swinging high.

Best of all, Eva had made up a song with him, and everyone had sung along.

5
Loop-de-Loop

Wednesday night after dinner, Jake swallowed his last bite of mint chocolate ice cream. He pushed aside his bowl. Mom was setting up a surprise on the table, as silently as a tiptoeing robber.

"Now!" Mom said.

The first thing Jake touched had a tiny knob on its top. Beneath that, he felt a rounded shape, like an upside down cup. As he picked up the knob, it dinged. Jake scanned the table with his other hand. Why, there were twelve little bells in a row! Each bell played a different note.

"Fantastic!" he breathed.

The tiny tags on the bells listed their musical notes, "a" through "g". One by one, as Mom read the notes, Jake carefully labeled them with Braille sticky tape. ˙ for "a". : for "b". ¨ for "c".

Jake cradled the lowest, biggest bell in his hand. "C" was a boring name, so he decided to call it Chris. He imagined Chris growing little arms and legs.

Water splashed at the sink. Pans clattered. The refrigerator opened. A moment later, he smelled peanut butter. "May I have sliced pickles on my sandwich?" he asked. Making his lunch for school was his chore, but he wasn't about to point that out.

"Pickles and *peanut butter*?" With a chuckle, Mom strolled over to kiss him on the top of the head.

Touching the brass bells in order, Jake named them Doug, Eve, and Faye. Each one was a little smaller. The next three became George, Ann and Blake. As he named them, he imagined them turning into bell people, sprouting arms and legs.

For the five higher notes, he chose names from *The Wizard of Oz*. The higher C sounded like a Cowardly Lion. Next, he chose Dorothy and Auntie Em. "F," he muttered, stuck.

"Foolish Toto," Mom suggested. "Milk or juice?"

"Milk." Jake rang the bell again. Ah, he had it now. "Floppy Scarecrow!"

The refrigerator closed with a clunk. "I'll be reading in the living room." Mom always told him when she left a room, so he wouldn't keep talking to the air. Jake's tiniest, highest pitched bell became Glenda, the Good Witch.

He rang a bell and listened intently, then rang another one. If the second bell was higher or lower, he could hear it. Yet no matter how many times he tried, he couldn't tell if a bell was Doug or George. Jake yawned as he played a scale. That's when he noticed that Ann rang like an angel. Next, he started giving each bell a personality. The biggest one, Chris, chimed for chocolate. Doug donged daringly.

"Five minutes," Mom called.

It couldn't be bedtime yet. *No way.* He rang Emma and hummed her note. She loved anything that started with an "e", like emails or elephants. Faye was funny. George gathered gold. Vaguely, Jake heard his mother's footsteps. Blake would be the bossy bell.

"Enough already," Mom cried, sliding the bells out of his reach. "Go to bed!" She shooed him out of the kitchen. Jake fell asleep imagining himself developing a new bell trick to show Brandon and Eva and Shaniqua.

*****

The next Saturday, Jake arrived late at the School for the Blind. Mom hadn't let him leave until he had finished cleaning his room. As he hurried down the hill from the parking lot, he could hear Katherine encouraging Eva to move faster. Why, he had completely missed the friendship circle!

Meredith scooped him up the moment he reached the bottom of the hill. Then she started talking. She talked about acting in a play last summer. She chatted about her dog, Buster.

Jake soon stopped paying much attention. The track's surface seemed springy, not the rip-all-the-skin-off-your-hand-when-you-fall type. Besides, his legs were beginning to learn the shape of the oval. A long straight stretch, and then a tight turn, followed by another straight stretch that led into a second turn. They walked a bit and ran a bit. Meredith yakked and yakked.

"There it was, my *big* moment," Meredith was saying when he started listening to her again. "Hundreds, *no thousands,* of people were in the audience. The hobos danced onto the stage. I was the third hobo in the second line, doing a *perfect* kick in my boots that were three sizes too big. Buster was onstage, too, since he was Annie's dog. With a loud bark, Buster pulled away from Annie. He jumped up and *kissed* me. Then he slurped every hobo on stage, one after the other, right down the line!!"

Jake had to admit it was a good story. He'd have to remember it to tell Dad next time he called. A big raindrop splashed on his arm.

"Ooh, I hate rain," Meredith said and sped up.

In the middle of their eighth lap, cold drops splattered on Jake's face. He didn't really mind. "Two ducks out splashing in the rain," he panted. "Two Adventure Sports ducks."

Mere didn't laugh, and she sure didn't slow down. Jake sighed. Maybe teenage girls didn't like ducks.

"Let's get this over with," Meredith muttered and dragged him into the next turn.

As the drizzle changed to a steady rain, Meredith trotted faster. Jake gasped and wheezed his way around the track. Cold drops trickled down the back of his neck inside his sweatshirt. He ran and ran and ran.

Seven laps later, Jake stumbled into his warm car,

shaking water out of his hair. Even his fingers felt exhausted from gripping the rope. Jake collapsed into his seat with a squelching sound. He might never be able to move his legs again.

"How about a bowl of chicken soup when we get home?" Mom asked.

Jake's stomach growled. Even his elbow shivered.

As usual, Mom sang as they drove away, "I'm singing in the rain. Just singing in the rain."

Jake leaned back, listening to her voice and the *drip drop, drip drop* on the roof. He might be tired, but he could still daydream. He hadn't added to his flying guide dog story in ages. First, he needed a good beginning...

Instead of taking a walk that spring day, Wagger would be taking a fly.

And Jake began to daydream...

Wagger would soar up into a damp cloud. Up, up, UP, he would go. Of course, Bert would be holding onto his harness. They'd pop out of the cold cloud into the warm sunlight. The white puffy cloud had turrets like a castle. "Woof, woof!" Wagger would bark, flying a loop-de-loop around a spire.

"Ha, ha!" Bert would laugh.

Jake spread one arm wide, pretending to fly around his car until he got another idea. He was starting to feel as if he really were Bert.

Taller...stronger.

With his super hearing, he heard a voice below him on the earth, crying, "Help!" It was a soft voice.

"Forward," he commanded with a flick of his wrist

for a hand-signal. Like an arrow, Wagger sped toward the cry. The dog's tail wagged a trillion miles an hour. He landed with a loud thump on a slanted surface. "Where am I?"

"Top my houthe," a tearful voice answered from about his waist. The little guy sniffled, then asked curiously, "Can't you thee?"

"Wagger has eyes enough for two of us," Bert replied. Jake wiggled his toes. He liked that line. *"Are you trapped up here?"*

"I cwimbed. Out my window," the kid announced. "Now I thtuck!" A tiny hand slipped into his. It was a warm, trusting hand.

"Tell you what," he said. "Since you're a good climber, you climb into my arms. Wagger will fly us both to the ground."

The small boy scrambled up him as if he were a tree. "Woo-eeee," the kid shrieked as Wagger flapped his tiny wings. All three of them glided to the ground.

Gently, he set the boy down. "Go on now. Find your mother."

The last thing he heard was the little boy crying, "Mama, Mama! Flying Wagger and the bwind boy thaved me."

With a yawn, Jake came back into the real world. Raindrops splattered on the roof. *Drip drop, drip drop.* He was finally warming up. His sweatshirt smelled like wet dog hair as it steamed dry.

His mother was singing softly now, "I'm singing and dancing in the rain."

6
The Three Stowaways

The next Saturday, the sun shone on his back and Meredith smelled flowery. Now and then, she sighed. She moved slowly, too. Last night had been her first high school dance, and she'd stayed up dancing past midnight.

That suited Jake just fine. He was trying to solve a mystery, a faint echo he heard now and then. If he stomped, he could make out a wispy sort of reverberation that bounced against his eardrums. Barely. When he asked Meredith, she grunted that they were passing the bleachers. After that, every time Jake heard the mysterious echo, he counted a lap.

Soon Eva walked by his side, as quietly as a wombat. Mr. Solomon had stayed home with a cold, so she didn't have a partner. Jake had googled wombat on his computer. It was a real animal, all right, a furry digging creature from Australia.

Early settlers had called them little bears. The animals made friendly pets, once tamed.

All three of them had finished their tenth lap, or maybe it was their ninth, when Meredith croaked, "There's that cat. Going into the basement of the building at the top of the hill."

Eva gasped. "Let's go up and explore!"

Jake added a bounce to his step. The rest of the kids *were* on the other side of the oval track.

"We shouldn't," Meredith objected.

"Bueno. The two of us will go by ourselves." Eva tugged on Jake's sleeve. "Right, Jake?"

Eva could see shapes and light. He hoped that would be enough. "Right." Jake dropped his end of the rope and reached for Eva's elbow. He caught her shoulder, his fingertips brushing her soft curls.

Together, they scrambled straight up the hill. It was so steep he had to touch one hand to the grass so he wouldn't slide backward. At the top, he whistled. Sure enough, he could hear the echo of a building ahead. *Very close.* He tugged on Eva's shoulder to slow her down. The two of them crept along.

Footsteps thumped up behind them. Jake caught a whiff of flowers. "Disappeared right about here," Mere panted. "Beats me where. There isn't a door."

Jake stood still, listening. At first he only heard Meredith's breathing. Then a bird sang in the distance. A squirrel scurried on the roof. Finally, he detected a wail...an itsy bitsy cry. There! He heard it again.

"Mew," a little voice wailed.

Feeling the ground with his feet, Jake shuffled

toward the voice. He didn't want to fall into anything. "Over here." If only he had his cane.

Someone touched his right hand. "Take my elbow," Meredith said, guiding him. Jake pulled her along. He led the two girls every step of the way.

"The cat's in the window well." Meredith stopped abruptly. "And *you* found her!" She thumped Jake's upper arm with her fist. "She's black with a white star on her chest. Ah, isn't she cute, Jake?"

What did she think, that he could see?

"Don't scare her." Eva's voice dropped lower in space as she crooned, "Here kitty, kitty."

Jake sank onto his knees in the grass beside Eva, holding his hands out in front of him. The cat meowed again. As its cry bounded closer, a shiver danced up his spine. He didn't know much about cats.

"She's skinny," Eva whispered.

"What do you suppose it's doing here?" Jake asked. "It sounds...lonely." Then the cat rubbed against his wrist. He jumped, but the fur felt soft, as soft as velvet. Now he understood how Eva had gotten the name for her cat. It started to rumble. "Ahh, he likes me." The cat's whole body shook in Jake's hands.

"Tst, tst, tst," Eva made an odd clicking sound. A singing gurgle emerged from her next, like a string of rolled r's.

With a yowl, the cat pranced out of Jake's hands. Everyone knew Eva could speak Spanish and English. It seems she could also speak *Catlish*. "The cat's a boy, not a girl," he argued, just for fun.

"Tame," Eva mused, ignoring him. "A wild cat

wouldn't let us this near." Then she oohed. "She's a girl, all right. She's nursing gatitos."

"Babies?" Meredith asked. Her voice became muffled, "You're right. There are two of the littlest kittens tucked under a piece of plastic in the window well. The bigger one has its eyes open."

The mother cat meowed, a loud drawn-out cry. Goose bumps rose on Jake's arms.

"Take it easy," Meredith exclaimed. "I won't hurt your..." Her voice shot up into a yelp.

The cat hissed, then rowled in rising fury. Jake imagined the cat slinking forward, ready to tear Mere limb from limb. With a moan, the older girl scurried back to his side, then leaned against his shoulder. *Great!* She was leading a wild cat right to him.

The spitting sounds stopped. Beside him, Meredith sighed in relief. On his other side, Eva murmured calmly, "Ten days to two weeks old."

"How do you know?" Jake asked.

"Porque," Eva answered.

"Because...?" Jake translated.

"That's when a kitten's eyes first open."

So one of the babies was just beginning to see. *Cats are born blind*, Jake realized. He took a deep breath, sitting back on his heels between the two girls. *Just like me.* The littlest one's eyes still weren't open.

"What's up, Cuz?" Brandon exclaimed from the track below. "What are you doing talking in the grass? We're supposed to be running."

"Right, no sitting!" Katherine called.

Jake swallowed. Brandon must have heard

Meredith's screech when the mother cat threatened to attack her. She did have an unmistakable shriek. The last thing the three of them wanted was to have The Boss up here with Socks. "Be down in a minute!" he shouted. Then he turned to the girls. "What do we do now?"

"Tell Katherine?" Meredith suggested hopefully.

"No way," Eva snapped. "She'd tell the groundskeeper, and who knows what he would do. The groundskeeper can't let kittens grow up at the School for the Blind."

Jake agreed. Cats and guide dogs were not a good mix. Just like his parents when they were married. "The kittens are our secret."

As the silence stretched, Jake wondered if Meredith would be any good at keeping secrets. She did like to talk *a lot*. He crossed his arms. "You can't tell anyone. Not even Brandon!"

"All right," the older girl agreed in a grumpy voice. "My lips are sealed. "

"Catch a lot of mice," Eva sang out softly to the cat in farewell. The mother cat yowled from the window well, just as if she understood her.

As they skidded back down the hill, Jake said, "We can think of the cats as stowaways. Like on a ship, a pirate ship." He imagined the students of the school singing pirate songs and pounding their canes on the floor while the teachers swung across the classrooms on ropes.

Grinning, Jake exclaimed, "The three stowaways at the School for the Blind!"

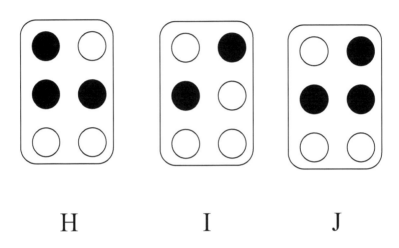

H   I   J

Now you know the first ten letters of the alphabet in Braille. Remember them! These ten letters are the key to learning the rest of the alphabet. Reading is like solving a puzzle, don't you agree?

7
Gummy Worms

Rain drummed on the cafeteria roof, and thunder boomed in the distance. Kansas was famous for its spring thunderstorms. If he were at home, he'd be sitting by an open window. Instead, he was stuck inside. "My pickle for your cupcake," he offered.

"Nope," Emily said without a beat of hesitation.

"My applesauce?" he asked.

This time she paused, yet when she spoke her voice sounded firm, "Forget it."

The drum of rain changed to a rhythmic pounding. *Was it hailing out there?* This storm was a whopper! Jake dropped his voice, trying to sound cool, like Brandon, "Corn chips for a cupcake?" All the good trades were long gone.

Her cupcake smelled *so* good.

"No spaghettio, Kidio," Emily replied.

It wasn't one of his favorite sayings. Running footsteps pounded behind their table, but Jake ignored them. He was too busy considering his next move. Before he could speak again, his cane slid off his lap.

"Got you, No Eyes!" a familiar voice hissed.

Desmond. Jake's heart dropped. The other boy laughed like a wild man, as if he were dancing around in a circle. Every student in the cafeteria must be listening. Jake bit down on his bottom lip. Usually, he ignored Desmond, but not this time. Without his cane, he couldn't get around school alone.

Jake stood up, his ears steaming. Desmond was the only kid in his class that he couldn't stand. Desmond had teased him since Kindergarten. Jake lifted one arm to protect his face and reached out with the other hand. Just as he opened his mouth to yell, Emily tugged on his sleeve.

"Tell him to go jump off a cliff," she suggested.

"A cliff?" Jake repeated. Gigantic drop-offs were frightening to him. Still, it was a funny image. He could imagine Desmond falling head over heels through the air, tumbling toward a lake. Jake laughed, dropping his arm.

A ruckus broke out in front of him and spread behind him. There were too many sounds to tell what was going on. Were kids wrestling? As he sat down beside Emily, a voice exclaimed, "Flying cane!" Jake thought it might be one of the fifth graders. Then he heard a collective gasp.

"Oh, no!" a boy cried.

"Duck!" yelled a girl as something landed on the

table in front of him with a clunk. The last of his milk splattered.

Emily groaned.

Pleased, Jake slid his cane onto his lap, clutching it firmly. He was just opening his mouth to thank his anonymous cane rescuer when the room fell completely silent. *Uh oh*, Jake thought.

"Is there a problem here?" a familiar voice asked. It was Ms. Tarantino, his old second grade teacher.

Beside him, Emily took a deep breath. "Ye…"

Jake poked her, and she stopped in the middle of the word. Kids like Desmond never bothered anyone when adults were around. He had a feeling it was time to solve this by himself. "No, Ma'am," he replied. "I... uh...lost my cane and someone...tossed it back to me."

Ms. Tarantino didn't move. Finally, she said, "If you say so, Jake."

As her high heels click-clacked away, Jake sighed.

Emily slid something toward him. "Want to split my cupcake?"

"Indubitably," he replied. That word was used in some musical or another, maybe *The Sound of Music*. He bit into his half. Sweet chocolate melted in his mouth. It tasted even better than he'd imagined. Jake licked his fingers. *Did girls always give boys food when they felt sorry for them?*

"What are you going to do?" Emily whispered.

Jake nibbled on the last of the cupcake. Desmond had always teased him, but he'd never done anything this bad. Jake searched for crumbs with a damp finger. If he had the power, he'd turn Desmond into a frog...or better yet, an ant. The cafeteria ladies hated ants. "Beats me," he answered.

*****

Every morning and every afternoon that week, Jake splashed across the schoolyard. Recess was inside, too, with Ms. Rose. Jake played checkers and stayed clear of Bully #1 – except for the time he heard Desmond heading into the hall for a drink and couldn't resist sticking out his cane.

"Missed him," Emily whispered.

Every night, amidst the crashing of thunder and the tingling smell of rain, Jake made up an adventure about Flying Wagger. Flying Wagger and the Blind Boy saved a five-year-old girl from a charging bull. Flying Wagger and the Blind Boy caught a teenager in midair when his parachute wouldn't open.

Friday night, the rain finally stopped. Jake yawned and stretched, considering his next flying dog story. As he wiggled his toes, he remembered Socks dragging Katherine up the hill at the Adventure Sport's practice. All young guide dogs made mistakes, right? Outside, a branch of the oak tree rattled against the house, and that gave Jake an idea...

Like any dog, Wagger would be chasing a squirrel at the park. Only, he would have an unfair advantage. Flippety-flappety, flippety-flappety, his wings would flutter as he swooped down on the chittering creature. The rodent would be freaked out of its bushy tail.

Bert would follow his dog, yelling, "Leave it!"

Jake imagined himself as Bert…

Taller…stronger…faster…

He ran as fast as he could, but it wasn't fast enough. The poor squirrel zipped up a tree and into a hole. Wagger was so excited that he hung in the air, his ears quivering and his tail spinning in circles. So he waved his arms and shouted, "Leave it!!"

Wagger obeyed.

And that's when things got much worse. The flying dog careened away from the tree toward a preschool birthday party at a nearby picnic table. Children screamed and ducked. All but the birthday boy. While the kid sat straight up, pointed hat on his head, Wagger snatched the hot dog right out of his hand.

Jake fell asleep to the pitter-patter of more rain, imagining that he was Bert, the brave daredevil who could face anything, the mighty adventurer whose guide dog was being a little bit bad.

*****

The next day, the very last practice on the track, Jake stole up the slippery hill before the Friendship Circle. Eva unwrapped a pork burrito she'd brought from home and set it down on the ground. While the mother cat gobbled up the snack, he and Eva lay on their bellies by the window well and reached in to pet the kittens. Jake wished he'd brought some food, too. He didn't think the mother cat would enjoy eating what he had hidden in his pocket.

Dampness seeped into his clothes as he lay on the damp grass. The little kittens were wobbling around now. Their fur felt softer than their mother's. *Like cotton balls.* Jake liked the smallest one the most. It wasn't any bigger than his hand, and its tail was bent.

"Come on," Eva sighed. "If we stay up here too long, everybody will get curious."

"Not to mention the dog," Jake agreed.

"You babies will be ready to leave your mama at the time of the Stagecoach Run. That's when we'll come back to save you." Eva half sang, "Y tú también, Mama cat." She ended with a rolling gurgle deep in her throat.

Jake stroked the cats one more time. Had the mother cat run away before she'd had her kittens and then been unable to find her way home? Or had people dumped her on purpose? The two babies were nursing. They purred, their bodies rumbling from tiny pointed ears to the tips of their tails. "See you in a month."

Since the hill didn't have trees, he slid down on the seat of his pants. Halfway down, he heard Eva gasp and slip, landing with a thud beside him. Jake began to roll. By the time he reached the bottom, they were both hollering. No wonder he liked Saturdays.

Jake tugged bits of wet grass out of his hair as they joined the gathering group. This was their last meeting at the School for the Blind. He leaned over to touch his toes. Not seeing the kittens every week would be awful. Jake crossed his ankles and hung down again. He didn't want to even think about the trail next Saturday. For a whole month, he'd avoided imagining all that gravel.

When they sat down to stretch, The Boss challenged them to jog 20 laps. Jake groaned and struggled to his feet. *Two miles?*

"Bet you can do it." Mere handed him the rope.

Jake had a sneaky suspicion a bet with Meredith would be painful. Side by side, they settled into a trot. "You're on," he agreed. Speaking softly, when he couldn't hear other footsteps, Jake told her about visiting the stowaways, how the babies' purrs had sounded like miniature motorboats, how mama cat liked Mexican food. To Jake's surprise, he ran three times around the track without his lungs aching.

On the fourth lap, he called, "Hey everybody, I have worms in my pocket. One for each of you!"

"Disgusting," Shaniqua replied from the other side of the track.

Good, Jake thought. She sounded as if she believed him.

As Shaniqua pounded to catch up with him, she added, "Rockets have carried worms into space, Whistling Boy. For experiments, you know." She slowed to a trot.

Jake sniffed. One of the things he liked most about Adventure Sports was the chance to get dirty. As usual, Shaniqua smelled clean, like shampoo. The older girl added, "That's one experiment not for me. Uh, uh! Dr. Shaniqua will *not* be studying worms."

"*Dr.* Shaniqua?" her college-aged partner, Adele, teased. "Tell me, Madam, what are you planning to study when you go to college? "

"Astronomy," Shaniqua replied. "Already told you that, girl."

"And you?" Adele's voice turned in his direction.

Jake couldn't tell if she was speaking to him or to

Meredith. He opened his mouth to say he wanted to open an ice cream store, but Meredith giggled and said in a show off voice, "Acting." Abruptly, she sounded serious, "Or maybe I'll be a vision teacher."

"Because of Brandon?" Adele asked.

Jake could feel Meredith shrugging all the way through the rope. He closed his mouth. This was getting interesting.

"So, how did he lose his sight?" Adele continued.

"An accident." For once, Meredith seemed reluctant to talk.

Jake didn't blame her. This was private stuff. Still, he hoped she wouldn't stop. He tried to keep from panting, so he could hear every word.

"Brandon was as skinny as a fencepost," Meredith whispered. "It was a fire...that burned down the garage. Bran was burned all over his body."

Jake shivered. The time he'd burned his hand on the stove his fingers had throbbed, keeping him awake. He couldn't imagine how horrible it would feel to throb all over.

"When they finally uncovered his eyes, he couldn't see," Meredith said. "Since then, he's had three operations grafting his skin and it's beginning to look normal. But his voice might never..."

Footsteps pounded up behind them. "Talking about me, cousin?" Brandon growled.

Jake sucked in air. He'd never thought to wonder why Brandon's voice might be deep and breathy. He'd just figured he wanted to sound cool.

"Sure thing," Meredith admitted, but she sounded

embarrassed.

"Pretty gruesome, huh?" Brandon snorted. They thumped along for half a lap in silence and then he said in a rush, "Do any of you Dudes wish you could see?" His voice cracked.

"Dudes?" Shaniqua repeated.

"Not usually," Jake answered honestly.

"Me, neither," Katherine said. That was the first moment Jake knew The Boss had caught up with them. He wasn't surprised. Katherine seemed to have a built-in radar for serious conversations.

"I do," Brandon whispered. He hesitated, and then squeaked, "All the time."

"That's because you remember," Katherine said gently.

Jake bit down on his lower lip, wishing he could do something, *anything*, to make his friend feel better.

"Jake and I were born blind, so we've never seen," The Boss continued. "And Shaniqua lost her sight as a baby. But you were *seven*, Brandon."

Jake felt a tugging on the rope, as if Meredith were trying to move closer to her cousin.

"Sometimes, seeing is *all* I think about," Brandon said in a strangled voice. Immediately, his footsteps pounded off into the distance. It took half a lap before Jake could breath right again.

Meredith didn't make a single sound until the galloping footsteps caught up with them again. "Oh, Cuz," she exclaimed. Her voice broke. "I..."

Brandon cut in, "Remember the time I hid grasshoppers in your bed?"

Jake could imagine Brandon doing that, *little skinny-as-a-fencepost boy.*

"I'm sorry I..." Meredith said in a rush.

Her cousin snickered, interrupting her again, "I was four, and you were seven." He demanded roughly, "Remember?"

Jake could have counted to ten in the silence.

"You were a dreadful little twerp," Meredith finally said. "But the grasshoppers were the worst. All scratchy, hopping around my toes." Her giggle joined Brandon's. Jake took a deep breath and joined in.

After that, whenever anyone passed, they talked about worms. Just worms. Mr. Solomon said he collected worms for fishing. Katherine told about feeling sorry for the worms in her big brother's worm farm and setting them all free in the garden.

At the end of practice, Jake was tired, but he felt good. Meredith had been right. He *could* run two miles. He handed the first gummy worm to Brandon, who was sitting on the bleachers snapping his fingers. It was a nice fat worm, about as long as Jake's hand.

"I've always wanted to eat a worm," Brandon said in his cool cat voice, smacking his lips. Jake put his palm over his own mouth to keep from laughing.

"Boys are *crazy*," Shaniqua grumbled, joining them. "I always knew that."

A wet nose snuffled at Jake's pocket. Katherine had arrived. The Boss pulled the dog away. Socks wasn't allowed to sniff people while he was working.

"What about me?" Eva begged. He handed her one, and she chewed noisily. "Yum."

Eva hadn't given away his secret either! Next, Jake gently touched Shaniqua's hand so he knew exactly where it was. "Want to hold a worm, Shaniqua?" He dangled a long worm over her hand, slithering the rubbery candy across her fingers.

For the first time ever, the older girl screeched, "Aaaahhhhh!" A second later, the worm was snatched out of his hand. "This isn't a real worm!" Shaniqua hollered.

Everyone laughed. Katherine's giggle sailed above the rest. Grinning, Jake handed out gummy worms. Everybody got one, even Katherine. She liked candy just as much as the children.

Walking up the sloping sidewalk toward the parking lot where his mother waited for him, Jake heard Eva call, "See you later, Jake."

Jake knew Eva must be thinking the same thing he was right now. She was wishing the little stowaways would be safe for the next month. Hoping there would be plenty of mice at the School for the Blind for mama cat to eat.

He had just opened his mouth to yell good-bye when he thought of the perfect nickname for his friend. Jake bounced his cane on its rubber tip. Wasn't Eva small? Quiet? Wasn't she furry, with her curly hair?

When he heard Eva's car rattling past him, Jake shouted, "After a while, Wombat!"

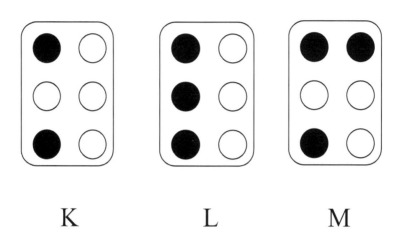

K   L   M

Here are the next three letters. Do you remember how to number the dots? K uses dot 1 and dot 3. Dots 1, 3 and 4 form the letter M.

Now, look at A, B, C again. How is the A different from the K? How is the B different from the L? Don't you love puzzles?

8
The Mighty Adventurer

On the first Saturday in April, Jake heard a truck rush past as he slid open the side door of his van. A motorcycle zoomed through the parking lot. The time had come for Adventure Sports to practice on the trail. Jake's throat had a lump lodged halfway down.

Of course, he'd had a lump in his throat since last Wednesday when Ms. Rose had called his mother to discuss *daydreaming during math*. He'd been positive his "crime" had been a perfect cloak and dagger operation, as Dad liked to say. Yet it seemed that Ms. Rose knew exactly when he was off in another world. Even worse, Mom had insisted that the two of them spend an hour every night studying division.

The lump in his throat was swelling to the size of a baseball...or maybe a basketball. Jake tried to swallow.

"Don't worry, Honey," Mom called, clicking off her choir tape as he stepped into the parking lot.

Jake slammed the car door. Mothers shouldn't be able to read a guy's mind. He searched for the curb with the sliding tip of his cane. At least the gang would be swimming at the indoor pool afterwards. He could look forward to that.

Familiar voices drifted toward him. Jake crossed the sidewalk and joined the circle on the grass. He didn't even hear what they were supposed to be sharing. He was too busy remembering his Running Monster. The creature had huge feet just perfect for tripping unsuspecting kids. And it would be a short, hairy critter that *loved* gravel...

"Jake? Do you have an idea for our team name?" Katherine urged.

"Name?" his voice shot up.

"So far, we have Adventure Sport Speedsters," Katherine said. "Roadrunners."

"And Starbursts," Eva added.

Jake blurted out the first idea that popped into his mind, "Flying Guide Dogs."

"Hey, that's pretty good!" Brandon slapped him on the back. "At the race, we *will* be flying."

"Next week, we'll vote on our team name." The Boss clapped her hands.

Uh oh. Jake knew what that meant.

"Three miles today," Katherine continued. "A mile and a half to the tennis courts, then return by the same route. Happy running, Adventure Sportsters!"

"A mile longer than last week?" Shaniqua

groaned. The other kids moaned along with her like a ghostly choir. Mr. Solomon started collecting canes to lock in the trunk of his car.

"Jake?" Eva touched his arm, whispering, "I'm working on Mama to let me make a bowl at the pottery shed at the School for the Blind." Jake leaned closer to hear. "*Maybe* I can sneak out to visit our cats. I'll keep you posted." Then she was gone.

"Ready?" Meredith asked, handing him the rope.

Fat chance, he thought, but he clamped his fingers around the knot. He and Meredith zipped across the busy street in a big group with the others. When they reached the trail, he slid his feet along, feeling for dips. The surface wasn't flat at all! There were holes everywhere. Not to mention, *tons* of gravel.

Jake heard the other kids' voices disappearing into the distance. *Hey, where was everyone going? Weren't they all going to run together? Like at the track?*

He ran faster but couldn't keep up, no matter how hard he tried. Meredith chattered about the clouds in the sky and the flowers. As if he cared about blue skies and yellow daffodils.

The trail curved back and forth in S-curves like a snake. They had to cross streets, and he didn't even have his cane. Oh, he was used to crossing streets with his mother. He held her elbow and trusted her. Mom wouldn't walk him off a cliff.

He wasn't so sure about Meredith.

Besides, the Running Monster might be waiting along this very stretch. Jake imagined the creature with his enormous tennis shoe stuck out in the middle of the trail. *A size twelve sneaker.* No, a size twenty-six! The hairy fiend would have three noses...

"You enjoy reading?" Meredith asked, yanking him out of his daydream.

Jake grunted.

She must have thought he meant *yes*. "Me, too." Meredith wasn't even panting. She rattled on, "I've been reading a fantasy about animals you might like. It's called *Redwall*."

Jake didn't want to talk.

Surely, they should have arrived at the tennis courts by now. The first mile and a half was lasting forever. Whistling didn't do any good. Counting steps didn't do any good. Even thinking about the stowaway kittens didn't help. At least, Meredith told him to step up every time they came to a curb.

"Where's your whistle, Whistling Boy?" Shaniqua called. She was running towards him from the opposite direction! *Whoosh*, her footsteps passed and she was gone. Could she be heading *back* already?

A minute later, Meredith yelled, "Brandon! Hey, hey, look at you. You're doing great, Frog Guy!"

"Run hard, Hairy Toes," Brandon replied. Then he added in his cool-guy voice as he pounded closer, "You, too, Jake."

Beside him, Meredith dissolved into giggles. "Last year, I read *The Hobbit* so many times my family teased me about turning into one. They said I'd grow bushy hair on my toes if I wasn't careful."

One by one, Adventure Sports' kids passed with the *thump-thump, thump-thump* of running footsteps.

Then softer paws padded toward him. Jake wished he had four legs. Running must be easier for a dog.

"You two okay?" The Boss asked as she and Socks changed direction to run alongside them.

"Sure," Meredith replied.

Nope! Not me! No way! Jake replied silently.

"I can hear you shuffling, Jake," Katherine said. "Lift your feet. It'll be easier."

"I am," Jake insisted and ran faster to prove it. Now each breath made his chest ache like fire.

"No, no, no," Meredith panted, tugging him back with the rope.

"Slow and steady. That's the trick," their fearless leader agreed cheerfully.

With a grateful sigh, Jake slowed down.

"Hey, don't walk!" Meredith exclaimed.

It didn't make any more sense to him than colors.

"See you later," Katherine said as she turned around to speed after the others with her guide dog. "Don't eat too much at the rest stop, Jake."

When they reached the halfway point, Jake slurped down two glasses of ice-cold lemonade. The Boss hadn't said a word about drinking.

"Help yourself to cookies," Katherine's mother said sweetly.

Just to be polite, he nibbled on two oatmeal raisin cookies with chocolate chips. Then his hand inched forward, as if it had a mind of its own. He scooped up three more cookies and bolted down every crumb.

When he and Meredith started running, Jake's stomach ached. *Ooohh.* By the time he'd run a hundred steps, he felt like he'd swallowed a basketball. And they were all alone.

Soon even Meredith stopped talking. The trail became his worst nightmare. He had no idea how far he'd gone or how much further he still had to run. Not like on the track, where he could count laps. Jake shuffled his feet. He kept imagining himself stumbling into a pothole, falling into nothingness. His head flopped back. He knew he wasn't moving any faster than a snail.

I'm not going to make it, he thought. Meredith let him sit down three times to rest.

When he finally arrived, Jake stumbled to a standstill on the grass, his knees wobbling and sweat dripping down his face. He was the very last person finished. *The youngest of all.*

The other kids circled around him. It was all Jake could do not to burst into tears. "Everybody is going to beat me!" he exclaimed.

Shaniqua humphed. "The only way you can lose this race, boy, is not to cross the finish line."

"That's the way I felt last year," Eva admitted.

"Come on, Buddy." Brandon punched his arm.

He heard a familiar car door closing. "Ready to go swimming?" Mom called cheerfully. His mother always sounded jolly when he was upset.

"I want to go home!" Jake snapped. Grabbing his cane, he climbed into the van and turned his back on the trail.

Jake, the mighty adventurer, had met his match.

9
By Order of Jake

Jake sat at his desk at school. Too bad he couldn't wave his cane like a magic wand and make the whole world skip Saturday. *By order of Jake, the award-winning magician, there would be only six days this week. Monday. Today. Then Wednesday, Thursday, Friday...and Sunday!*

Fiddling with his cane, Jake thought about the board up in front of him with Ms. Rose's big desk to the side. He'd memorized every single inch of this classroom, down to the box of tissues on the nearest corner of the teacher's desk. The door was off to his right, and to his left was a long window ledge, big enough to sit on. Directly behind him, three desks back, was the art cupboard. He wasn't likely to trip here, but if he did, he'd have a pretty good idea where he'd be nose-diving.

School was *known* space.

Ever since the Outdoor Sports practice he had been reading, lying upside down on his couch with his feet hooked over the top. Yesterday after school, he had turned the last page of *The Lion, the Witch, and the Wardrobe.*

Before he could think about gravel, he'd switched on his computer. *What I Want to Be When I Grow Up*, he'd typed. The paper wasn't due for a week. Still, he'd written a page about inventing new flavors at an ice cream parlor, another whole page about designing video games for visually impaired kids, and finally a third page about writing Flying Wagger stories. Then he had fallen into bed, exhausted.

Down the hallway, Jake heard the school band playing *Seventy-Six Trombones.* The trombones were so far out of tune his toes curled. Not even the idea of playing Marco Polo with the three "J" brothers tonight could cheer him up. For the first time since the practice, Jake allowed himself to remember the trail...

Giant holes. Squealing cars. Knee-scraping gravel.

Instantly, his insides tied themselves into a square knot. It was all he could do not to gasp. Surely, the cars hadn't squealed like sick elephants! The palms of his hands felt damp with sweat. There was one thing he knew was real. He couldn't memorize the trail like this classroom. No matter how hard he tried.

The trail was *unknown* space.

He hated to admit it, but running on that path terrified him out of his socks. It was a hundred times worse than the hour of math with Mom every night. He drummed his fingers on his desk. The trail was miles and miles of unknown space. No way could he go back there next Saturday.

He just wished he knew how to tell his mother.

Mom wouldn't skin him alive. Jake sighed. No, her reaction would be worse. She'd say, "Jake," in her *Oh-my-goodness* voice with a hint of choked-up-ness. She'd be disappointed in him. And she was already upset enough about his daydreaming during school, the *Division Disaster*.

Beside him, he could hear Emily scribbling. She liked using her thick pencil for math, the one with the yarn dangling off the top. For the first time all year, he had finished his math problems faster than Emily. That's because Ms. Rose had announced a break from division. This week they were studying the proper way to count change. Jake rubbed the ridges on the edge of a quarter with his thumbnail. He was the only kid in the class who got to use real coins.

Another advantage to being blind, he thought.

Quickly, Jake ducked his head under his desk. He'd never tried his coin trick on linoleum before. He shouldn't, especially during math. Still, it would make him feel better. Jake dropped his nickel on the linoleum floor.

The nickel made more of a *plunk* than a *clank*, a heavier, ringing sort of sound. Two more times he let the nickel fall onto the linoleum, to fix the pitch in his ear. Then he dropped the quarter. The sound was heavy still, but the pitch was a little higher.

The penny and dime sounded similar to each other, but lighter, more of a *clink-a-link*. Telling the small coins apart was always the hardest.

"Jake?" Emily asked. "What are you doing?"

Jake sat up so fast that he bonked his head on the underside of his desk. "I..." He could feel his face blushing, so he started blathering, "Did I tell you we aren't rollerblading anymore at Adventure Sports? We're running, practicing for The Stagecoach Run."

"Daddy runs that race every year," Emily said. Her chair creaked, like it always did when she swung her legs. "Isn't it *miles* long? You must be crazy!" Still, she sounded impressed. "Hey, I'll be there. I'll cheer for you."

Jake rubbed the back of his head. Now Emily would be expecting to see him at the race.

"Don't be bashful, Jake," she whispered, poking him with the fuzzy end of her pencil. "Uh...what were you doing under your desk?"

On a whim, he decided to tell her the truth. "I'm memorizing the sounds of falling coins."

"Nobody can do that," Desmond jumped in. "Not even *bashful* Jake."

Had Bully #1 heard their whole conversation? Jake chewed on his lip. He'd had the rotten luck of having the only kid in the whole class he didn't like sitting behind him *all year*. "I can, too!" Jake cried.

"Now, children," said Ms. Rose warned.

Jake swallowed. Sometimes his teacher sneaked up on him. He made a split second decision, as his dad liked to say. "Please, Ms. Rose," he begged. "I've been working on a trick I'd like to show the class."

His Braillewriter whirred loudly as she tugged his

paper free. "First things first, young man," she barked, like a football coach. "Did you finish your math?"

"Yes, Ma'am," he replied. "Every problem."

"Let's see." She leaned in closer. "What's your answer to this first one? Three...?"

Ms. Rose couldn't read Braille very well, especially numbers. Braille used the first ten letters of the alphabet for numbers. So, A with a number symbol in front of it was 1. B was 2. C was three. Usually, an assistant, called a para, would print his answers above the Braille before he turned in his assignments to Ms. Rose.

His fingers danced over his paper as he read his answer, "Thirty-five cents. If the pen costs sixty-five cents, and the customer pays a dollar, you hand him a dime and a quarter."

He scooped up his coins. "The second answer is sixty-seven cents. If I were a shopkeeper, and the candy cost thirty-three cents, I'd start by giving the customer back the little coins. Like this!" With a satisfying jingle, he counted the coins out on his desk. "Thirty-four. Thirty-five. Next, would come the nickel. Forty." He plunked the dime down on his desk. "Fifty. Then, a quarter. Seventy-five. And the second quarter, one dollar!"

"That's correct, Jake," the teacher said, sounding a little surprised.

He snapped open the face of his Braille watch. Gently, he felt the tiny hands and the dots around the circle. "We have five minutes until recess." Now and then, Ms. Rose squeezed in a Show and Tell before they went outside. But she never let them beg.

He heard her soft chuckle. Ms. Rose raised her voice, "Jake wants to share a trick with us, class. Your attention up front please."

Standing up, Jake unfolded his cane with a practiced flick of his wrist. He strolled to the front of the room, rolling the ball on the tip of his cane from side to side. That way, he wouldn't trip over any chair legs.

Jake handed the teacher his coins. "Drop a coin for me, Ms. Rose?" he asked in a clear voice, like a real magician. He'd imagined this moment over and over. What he hadn't imagined was his stomach turning cartwheels. He breathed deeply. "Any coin, Ma'am. We'll do it ten times."

One at a time, Ms. Rose dropped the coins, while Emily agreed to pick them up, and Will kept score on the board. Jake missed the very first one. Still, he kept going. He got the next four correct and could hear the quiet deepening in the room. That meant his classmates were listening, too.

Plunk went the sixth coin, a high *plunk*.

The seventh coin was a nickel.

Clink-a-link. "A dime," Jake guessed, but he was wrong. The ninth coin was a penny, again. Finally, he knew the sound.

Coin number ten was the last quarter.

When Will and Emily announced, "Eight correct, two wrong," the whole class clapped. Everyone began to cheer! Jake bowed, wishing he had a velvet cape to flourish, a real magician's cape.

Ms. Rose let Jake choose three Jolly Ranchers, then slipped one of her rose shaped Tiptop Student awards into his hands. "This is for Outstanding Listening Skills, Jake," the teacher said quietly.

For the first time since she had called his mother about his daydreaming during math, he knew for sure that Ms. Rose was pleased to be his teacher. A warm rush of relief washed over him.

Jake ripped away the sticky backing on his Tiptop Student Award and stuck the rose on his desk next to his nametag. He couldn't wait to tell Mom. She believed in awards. And Ms. Rose didn't give them very often. This was his first all year.

"Big deal," Desmond muttered, but Jake ignored him. Bully #1 couldn't ruin this moment.

Jake popped a Jolly Rancher into his mouth. *Cherry, yum!* He imagined hurrying off the bus this afternoon and finding his mother in the kitchen. When she heard the news, she would give him a huge hug.

That would be the perfect moment to tell her about the trail, too. Maybe she wouldn't skin him alive when he refused to go to Adventure Sports. After all, he was an award winning kid.

Maybe she wouldn't even be disappointed in him.

Right. Jake folded up his cane. And his room would be filled from floor to ceiling with cherry Jolly Ranchers, too. Better yet, a huge, live Saint Bernard would be snoring on his bed.

Too bad he wasn't a real magician...

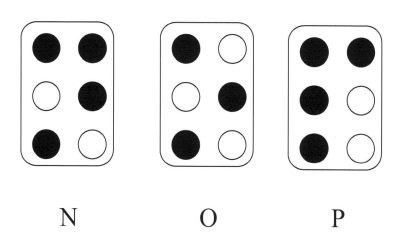

N   O   P

Reading Braille requires a light sense of touch. After a child learns the alphabet, she must learn to recognize how clumps of letters feel together. In other words, she or he must learn to read words.

10
Saturday at Home

Sunshine warmed his toes. Sparrows chirped. Jake sat up, swinging his feet over the edge of the bed. Saturday had arrived, the best day of the week! Halfway through a big stretch, Jake froze. No scheming with Eva about kittens today. No chasing Brandon. No listening to Shaniqua talk about outer space.

Usually on Saturdays, he slid into the kitchen on his socks. This morning he trudged past the stove. Mom kissed him on the head and continued singing, "I could have danced all night." *My Fair Lady* was her favorite musical. *Crack. Crack!* Mom broke the eggshells on the frying pan.

Last night, the two of them had been laughing, right here at this table. He'd survived the first of Ms. Rose's division tests, so they had been celebrating. Jake sat down, remembering...

"You aren't the only person in this family who likes to be creative, you know," Mom had announced, setting a cup of hot chocolate in front of him. "I hope to be using my imagination when I'm a hundred and five!" Then she'd acted out a story about herself as an old lady, singing and dancing while she bought groceries, stealing other people's carts because she wasn't paying attention. Getting herself into awful trouble. Jake had laughed so hard he'd choked on his hot chocolate.

Mom plunked his breakfast on the table in front of him. "Ta DA!" she exclaimed. She'd reacted just the way Jake had expected when he'd told her he wasn't going to practice. She had been disappointed in him.

For fifteen minutes.

After that, she had gone silent. Since then, she hadn't mentioned The Stagecoach Run *once*. Usually she talked about his choices that she didn't agree with over and over. Jake picked up his fork and tried to eat, but his eggs tasted like rubber.

He slunk back to his room and flipped on his computer. The mechanical voice greeted him. Jake typed P for programs, then H for his favorite computer game. Next, the voice said, "Human Body Adventure." Jake hit enter. He liked pretending to travel inside the body in the little spaceship, clicking the arrow buttons as he swooped along the blood vessels. White blood cells that could eat his spaceship beeped in warning. After a few minutes, he was tired of being inside the stomach and the heart. Even the brain seemed boring today.

Jake switched to his storytelling program. Maybe he'd write a story about Flying Wagger and Bert. The fearless pair could be competing in The Guide Dog Olympics. *Flying Wagger*, he typed, but his fingers didn't want to work right. He hit the up arrow so the computer would speak his typed words back to him.

"Flying wa-ter," the voice repeated.

He tried typing again.

"Fly in, waf-fle," the computer said this time.

"Oh, forget it!" Jake cried and switched it off.

He stood up and strode to the door, clicking open his watch. By now, the other kids at Adventure Sports would be meeting in the Friendship Circle. As Jake paced, he wondered what they were sharing. Maybe their best present of all time. If he were there, he'd talk about the giant stuffed dog Dad had sent him from California. St. Bernie took up half his bed.

Jake threw himself down beside the Saint Bernard, landing on his new copy of *Redwall*, the book Meredith had suggested. Jake sighed. He couldn't believe it. He was missing a teenage girl.

He opened the book to read. Within two sentences he found himself thinking about the kittens at the School for the Blind. If only he could know for sure that they were safe in their window well, that Eva had visited them. He wondered how the kitten with the crooked tail was doing. He was such a little squirt. In fact, Squirt would be a good name for him.

"I'm running an errand," Mom said from his doorway. Jake closed his book and hopped to his feet. Anything was better than sitting around wondering what he was going to do all day.

"You'll be fine here," Mom continued cheerfully. "I'll carry the cell phone. Call me if you have any problems." She had insisted that it was time he got used to being alone, a half an hour at a time. Jake sank down on his bed, listening to her footsteps grow softer down the hallway. "Have fun reading, Darling," she called. The front door clicked shut.

For the first time in his life, he was disappointed not to be going shopping. Ah well, he could pretend to be an explorer. That's what he normally did when he was alone. Jake headed for the kitchen, the *dark woods* of his house, and pulled the honey bear out of the cupboard. His mother didn't think honey bread was a good snack.

Then again, Mom wasn't here.

He squirted three mountains of honey on the bread and one on the counter. *Ooops.* With a swipe of his finger, he cleaned up the mess. Munching his honey sandwich, he climbed up to sit on the tabletop. Mom wouldn't allow this either. Not in her kitchen. Still, sitting up high kept him safe from the wild animals that lived in the deep woods.

Jake scooted his bells out of the way, arranging them in a row beside him, from lowest to highest. He rang each one. Bossy Blake and Funny Faye weren't as comical as usual. Last of all, Jake shook Glenda, the Good Witch. Then he rested his chin on one fist. Brandon would be finished running by this time. Eva must be about halfway back.

Abruptly, he remembered what Wombat had said

last week when he'd been so upset at the end of practice, "I felt the same way last year."

And *she* hadn't quit.

Jake passed Glenda, the Good Witch back and forth between his hands. *Ding, ding-ding.* Eva had been his age last year. *Ding, ding-ding.* If he quit now, the other kids would think of him as the boy who gave up.

Well, maybe not.

The tiny, highest pitched bell felt gooey from honey. Jake set it down and licked one sticky thumb.

He'd been willing to practice at the track because he wanted to be with his friends. Jake had a suspicion Katherine would say there was a more important reason for doing the Stagecoach Run.

Jake scooted off the table, his gummy hand adhering to the back of a chair. Then he slid on his socks to the sink, whizzing past an imaginary bear in the deep woods.

Katherine said she still fell down, and she was grown up. *Imagine, crashing into nothingness for* **twenty** *years!* he thought as he scrubbed his hands. The Boss was the most amazing grownup he knew. Every week she tried new things, like square dancing. She'd even raced in a triathlon.

If he grew up like The Boss, he might still fall down years from now. Maybe even when he had a guide dog of his own. If he grew as tall as Dad, he might still fall.

That meant he'd better get used to it.

The water on his hands steamed hotter. To tell the

truth, he didn't think he could ever get used to nose-diving in strange places. No matter how old he grew. Jake felt his hair standing up on the back of his neck as he contemplated the trail...

Giant pot holes big enough to swallow a boy.
Chunks of pointy gravel stabbing his knee.
Cars jumping curbs to race toward him.

He shook himself. He was letting his imagination get carried away. *Again!* Carefully, Jake dried one hand on his shirt.

Then he had his worst thought yet.

He couldn't spend every minute of his life in places he could memorize. He couldn't hang out at home all the time…or at school. *Could he?*

He was suddenly sure of one thing.

He didn't want to be a kid who stayed home on Saturdays because a new adventure grew too hard. *Too difficult to even try more than once.* He didn't want to stay home on Saturdays and play it safe with his computer and his bells.

Sliding past an imaginary moose, Jake climbed back up on a chair and sat down on the tabletop with a thump. Even if he ran as slowly as a three-legged turtle, he'd return to the next Adventure Sports practice. He'd return to the trail.

It was time to prove to *himself* that he wasn't a scared sort of guy…

11
Flying Wagger Strikes Again

Thursday after school, Jake waited at the usual spot, the last lamppost on the circle drive. It hadn't been a great day. During math Desmond had told a joke about a parrot. When Jake started laughing, Desmond had become very quiet. And Ms. Rose had lectured Jake for making a ruckus! When he'd tried to tell his teacher about Desmond, she'd said his behavior was *his own responsibility*.

As he jumped into the car, Mom called, "Greetings, son of my life!" Abruptly, she turned right instead of left. Even more odd, she didn't ask about his day. After two lefts and a right, Mom clicked off the engine.

When Jake opened his door, he smelled the asphalt of a new parking lot. "Where are we?"

"Wouldn't you like to know?" Mom teased, offering him her elbow.

They crossed a big parking lot, walked down steps and pushed open heavy double doors. When the doors swung shut behind them, the building was silent. *Hushed.* He couldn't even hear voices. "A library?" he guessed.

"Not even close," his mother said, clearly enjoying herself. The clicking of her heels echoed around them. As Mom opened another door, the sound of a pealing bell greeted him.

Jake stumbled to a stop.

A second bell donged. *Sweetly.* It sounded fuller than his bells at home. Mom grabbed his hand and dragged him across the room. "I want you to meet Mr. O'Shanigan, Jake. He's a bell ringer for St. Ann's Cathedral."

"Bell ringer?" Jake squeaked. He knew about trumpet players, but he'd never heard of a bell ringer.

"This is your first of three lessons," his mother announced. She nudged him. "Where are your manners, young man?"

Since his tongue was tied in knots, Jake held out his hand. Mom was giving him a gift when he'd messed up his math? When he'd skipped an Adventure Sports practice? When his tenth birthday was still weeks and weeks away?

Mr. O'Shanigan clasped his hand tightly.

"See you in half an hour," Mom said, patting Jake's shoulder. Her click-clacking footsteps receded before he could manage to say a single word. The door thumped shut, leaving him alone with the man.

"I understand you're a bell ringing fellow," Mr.

O'Shanigan said in a soft, deep voice. "Like me."

In that instant, Jake knew he could never confuse Mr. O'Shanigan with anyone else. His voice sounded like a melody – halfway between talking and singing.

"Yes, sir." One by one, Jake rang the hand-bells as Mr. O'Shanigan instructed. They must be four times the size of his bells at home, and each one had a wooden handle sticking straight up from its top.

Gently, Jake wrapped his fingers around the man's hand so he could feel the proper wrist action. On about the twentieth try, his wrist loosened, and the bell pealed freely. The sound reverberated in waves to fill the room. "It sings!" Jake cried.

"That it does, lad," Mr. O'Shanigan agreed. When he showed him how to stop the sound by holding a bell against his chest, Jake felt as if the music continued to sing inside his own body.

*****

On Saturday, Jake bounded toward the gathering circle. "Jake the mighty adventurer returns!" he cried. It seemed like forever since he'd seen the Adventure Sports gang. With a fiendish laugh, he challenged Brandon to a sword fight.

"En guarde!" Brandon exclaimed. Clicking and clacking their canes, the two boys circled each other.

"Not if you wish to stay alive, gentlemen," Katherine warned firmly.

Jake lowered the tip of his cane. Just once, he wished their fearless leader didn't hear every little thing that happened near her. He took a deep, happy breath as he and Brandon joined the Friendship Circle.

His thoughts whizzed around like a spaceship. Weeks ago, Brandon had talked about wanting to see. Jake had to admit that he was curious, too, especially about seeing his own face. Mom had said that Dad used to be as cute as a movie star when they had first fallen in love.

Still, his sighted friends, like Emily and the "J" brothers, couldn't hear the way he could. And Jake liked that. He liked it a lot. His friends considered his hearing almost magical. Maybe he could have a magic switch on his shoulder that he could flick on whenever he wanted to see. Then, when he wanted things back to normal, he could switch it right back off.

"Last practice, Roadrunners," Katherine announced. "Saturday morning at ten everyone is invited to my house to decorate shirts for the race."

Roadrunners, Jake repeated in his mind. He'd never been part of a team before.

"Next Sunday is the Stagecoach Run," The Boss continued. "Remember, we will be running on the street, not the trail. Believe me, half of the town will be there, so it will be *very* crowded. People will bump into you by accident. I want you to be prepared. My friend, Sandra, and I are going to run together, like last year." Jake thought he heard laughter in her voice. "We will be the official bumpers today."

The boss stayed silent for a moment. Then she added thoughtfully, "As a good luck gift to your teammates, I want each of you to share something about yourself in our circle that no one else knows."

People shared things from model car building to

playing the violin. When Shaniqua admitted she adored eating octopus, the circle groaned.

Jake flapped the bottom of his shirt to create a breeze. Even in the shade, his skin sizzled.

"I climb trees with my cat, Velvet," Eva admitted.

"Brandon here. I like to..." The older boy cleared his throat, and then growled in his deepest voice, "I like to cook. Spaghetti. Chocolate chip cookies."

Jake was impressed. The *What's-up-Dude* liked to cook.

"Your turn." Brandon poked him in the ribs with his elbow. "And don't tell them about your coin trick. I already know about that."

That's exactly what he'd been about to share. "Uh..." On impulse, Jake decided that if Brandon and Eliza and Shaniqua could share something private, so could he. "I make up stories. You know, I daydream."

"About what?" Brandon asked.

Jake rocked from his heels to his toes. "Flying Wagger. A guide dog with wings." He heard scattered laughter.

"That's how you got your idea for our team name, isn't it?" the older boy said.

"Maybe you can tell us a flying guide dog story at our campout this summer," The Boss suggested.

With that, the Friendship Circle was over. While they stretched, Jake imagined standing in front of a campfire telling about the time when Wagger caught a baseball at the World Series. Brandon would be so impressed that he would invite Jake over to his house to hold his frogs.

Or maybe he should tell the tale he'd made up last night about a family on vacation. When the baby walked over the edge of Niagara Falls, Wagger caught the baby's diaper in his teeth and saved the day.

"Missed you last week, Jake," Meredith said, slipping one end of the rope into his left hand.

Jake wasn't about to admit he'd missed her, too. "I'm reading *Redwall*," he replied as they hurried across the road in a mob. It was the hardest book he'd ever read. Mom had checked out a print copy from the library. Every night, they took turns reading aloud.

After their hour of math.

He could divide by single numbers now without manipulatives. To his surprise, he even understood remainders. Mom had created a new motto that she repeated every night, *"Listen Up, Sir Boy, and Ye Shall Learn."* She'd brailled the saying onto sticky tape and stuck it to the cover of his math book. Since none of his school friends could read Braille, it was a secret note. Mom might not know it, but Sir Jake wore armor and carried a shield with a fire-breathing dragon on the front.

He and Meredith reached the trail just behind Shaniqua and Adele. Jake scooted his feet through the first of the gravel. Already, the rope slipped a little in his sweaty fingers.

"Don't you love the animals that live at Redwall Abbey?" Meredith asked.

Cautiously, Jake began to jog. "My favorite is Matthais." The little mouse wanted to be a warrior, but no one took him seriously since he was so young.

"Uh oh!" Meredith sounded alarmed.

"Beep, beep," Katherine sang out.

Something jostled Jake's shoulder.

"Goodness!" The Boss exclaimed. "I'm SO sorry." She bumped into him again, harder this time, sending him crashing sideways into Meredith.

"Hey!" Jake stumbled to catch his balance as Katherine's high-pitched giggle danced away into the distance. *So that's what The Boss meant about being an official bumper.* Then he had a diabolical idea. "Where's Shaniqua?"

"Not far in front of us," Meredith whispered. She and Shaniqua might be one grade apart, but they were exactly the same age.

"Let's catch her." Jake sped up, lifting his feet.

Meredith dragged him faster with the rope. Now he could hear the *pat-pat* of footsteps.

"I want to walk on Mars when I grow up," Shaniqua was saying.

Jake tried to whistle. He hoped Shaniqua was too busy to notice. Still, it seemed fair to give her a hint that he was about to strike. Jake stretched out his right hand and shoved her shoulder. "Got you!" he roared and dashed away. Meredith howled with laughter.

"Flattened!" Shaniqua bellowed. "That's what you two will be."

The backs of Jake's legs burned. His lungs burned, too. Pounding footsteps gained on them.

"My shoelaces are flapping," Shaniqua drawled, veering in front of him. "I'd better tie them…right now." And she stopped dead.

Jake crashed into her. Shaniqua was softer than a brick wall, but not much. Beside him, Meredith groaned.

The first two miles of the run slipped by with stops and bumps and jostles. It was more fun than the time he had played bumper cars at the amusement park and Mom had let him drive.

By the break, he and Meredith were alone again. Jake sipped a small glass of lemonade and nibbled one cookie. He didn't allow his wiggling fingers to reach for more.

When he started running again, sunshine beat down on him. His arms drooped. *Scrape, scrape* shuffled his feet. Even his knees felt weak. Soon, his whole body dragged. Sweat dripped off his forehead. He felt as hot as if he were running through flames.

When his head started to roll from side to side, a nasty voice in his mind hissed, *Watch out! Whatever you do, don't fall.*

So, he began to daydream. He was an expert daydreamer, after all.

Jake imagined Flying Wagger and Bert flying around him in a circle. Wagger's little flapping wings would cool him off like a fan. The breeze would blow his sweaty hair off his forehead.

Then Jake imagined himself as Bert...

Taller...stronger...faster...handsome...

He put out his free hand and caught hold of Wagger's harness, cheering as they rose into the air. He and the dog of his dreams would FLY the last two miles. One by one, they flew past the others until he heard Katherine's voice beneath him.

He gave Flying Wagger the "fly lower" hand-signal. Careful not to make a peep, he swooped down nearer Katherine's head. "Flying Wagger strikes again!" he yelled. The Boss squealed in surprise and jumped as he fluttered past.

"Step up," Jake heard with a tiny part of his mind.

Flying Wagger rocketed toward the end. He leaned forward to get a firmer grip on the harness. Today, he wouldn't be last. He'd be the first person finished.

Then he stubbed his toe.

Jake tumbled out of his daydream to find himself diving forward. With a yelp, he clung to the skinny little rope. He reached out with his other hand as he stumbled. *Into nothingness.* Gravel brushed his fingertips. Panting, he hurtled to a stop.

"That was close." Meredith touched his elbow. "Are you all right?"

Except for his heart that was bouncing around in his chest like a panicked frog again. Jake stood up straight, so relieved that he hugged himself. He laughed, "Sure."

"Right before you tripped, you yelled something about flying water," Meredith said as she started walking.

He must have spoken aloud in his daydream. "Flying *Wagger*," Jake muttered, "not water."

"Ah," his partner said. "Your flying guide dog."

Jake shrugged. "I was daydreaming about flying to the end instead of running."

To his surprise, Meredith giggled. "If that imaginary guide dog of yours is strong enough to carry two, I vote we fly to the *beach* to cool off."

Jake stretched out his stride. Just because he'd had enough running for the day didn't mean he had to walk like a turtle. "What about Flying Wagger taking us to a waterpark?"

"Heavenly!" Meredith exclaimed. "I'll drift on an inner tube in a pool and listen to music."

Jake snorted. Sunbathe instead of speeding down a hair-raising slide? He would *never* fathom teenage girls. Still, he was beginning to understand Meredith. She liked being comfortable and reading a good book. Not to mention, acting dramatic.

"Do you believe in good luck charms?" his partner asked, interrupting his thoughts. Before he could answer, she rushed on, "I made you something for the race. Since I can't be at Katherine's next Saturday I wanted to give it to you today." She put a tiny bundle into his free hand. "I wear mine for big tests."

Jake stopped so he could feel it with both hands. Three strands of soft yarn had been woven together to make a little rope about six inches long. "Thanks," he said, dangling whatever-it-was in the air.

"It's a bracelet, Silly," Meredith teased. "Do you want me to tie it on tightly so you have to wear it all the time or loosely so you can take it off?"

A bracelet? "Loosely," he croaked.

"Don't worry. I made yours in guy colors," Meredith said, knotting it around his wrist. "It's orange and black to match our race T-shirts."

Jake spun the soft yarn around on his arm. Never in a million years would he have expected Meredith to give him a good luck charm. Let alone, *make* him one. He couldn't think of anything to say.

She tugged him back into a fast walk. "Come on, Lazybones." Walking back took them forever, but they made it, safe and sound.

The instant he and Meredith arrived, Eva dragged him off to the side. "I've got to go. Mama's waiting." Then she whispered, "Meet me next Saturday at noon. At the School for the Blind."

"Operation Save the Kittens," Meredith added over his shoulder.

Jake had nearly forgotten that he and Eva had agreed ages ago to rescue the cats on the same weekend as the Stagecoach Run. "Did you go to the pottery shed? Did you check on them?"

"No such luck," Eva replied.

So they didn't even know if the kittens were all right. Jake squeezed Eva's arm. "See you there," he promised. "Twelve sharp!"

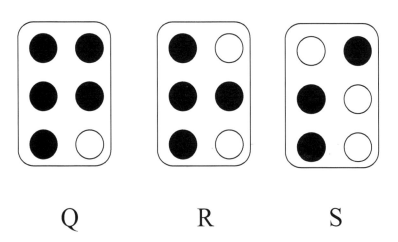

Q   R   S

Braille cells are very small in books. Imagine trying to feel all of the tiny dots as your fingertips race across a page.

Some people think learning to read Braille is harder than learning how to read print. What do you think?

12
Soggy Sock

Sir Jake the Handsome was about to knock Squire Desmond the Deadbeat off his horse, when Ms. Rose announced, "Today, we are going to do an experiment which focuses on our senses." Jake waved goodbye to his daydream and listened. "You'll guide each other quietly around our room and the hallway in pairs," the teacher continued. "One of each pair will pretend to be blind. Jake, will you teach us the proper way to be a guide, please?"

"Sure." Jake made his way to the front of the room. "Close your eyes, Ms. Rose," he ordered. "You're blind, remember?"

The class laughed.

When they grew quiet, Jake said, "Never guide a person like this." He held onto Ms. Rose's shoulder and pushed her along in front of him.

"Wait!" said Ms. Rose. "I can't…"

"See, it's scary," Jake said. "Instead, lead the way with your own body." He held out his left arm. "Please take my elbow, Ms. Rose. No, don't clutch it. Hold on loosely and trust me."

She snorted.

Jake walked slowly down the center aisle. "See, your visually-impaired friend follows half a step behind you. Leave extra space on that side. If you walk too close to things like desks, your partner will…" He waited. Sure enough, he heard a thump.

Ms. Rose groaned. Jake took a step to his right to give her space. It meant he was close to the desks, but he could handle that with his cane. "Always warn your partner if there is anything to trip over, like a hole or a pile of books." Ms. Rose's grip loosened as she relaxed. They reached the back of the room.

"Thank you, Jake." Ms. Rose broke away from him. "I have several blindfolds. When I hand you yours, tie it on tightly. No cheating, please. Desmond, come back here so you can be Jake's partner."

Jake barely kept himself from gasping.

"He doesn't need a blindfold!" Desmond cried.

"That's why *he's* going to be the guide, and *you* are going to wear the blindfold," Ms Rose said.

That shut him up.

"You two go on out in the hallway." She raised her voice, "For the first few minutes, class, concentrate on getting around. Then, try focusing on your other senses."

As he left the room, Jake heard everyone else milling around. He was glad Ms. Rose had sent them out first. It would be easier for him to guide in a place where there weren't tons of people. Beside him, he could hear Desmond's breathing.

Jake sucked in a deep breath of his own. "Blindfold on?" He could knock Desmond into the water fountain or the recycling bin. Even better, he could lead him to the top of the stairs.

The choices were endless.

Ms. Rose click-clacked up to them. "Desmond, let me help you tie that bandana so it's tight enough."

"Don't try anything," Desmond warned as she walked away.

"Who me?" Jake asked. He took the first step down the hallway. The moment for revenge had arrived.

Beside him, the taller boy clutched his arm, just the way he did Meredith's arm when they crossed the busy street at the beginning of the trail. Before he could stop himself, Jake veered out so they would both miss the water fountain.

It was too bad. The fountain would have caught Bully #1 right in the stomach. When he knew he was somewhere near the end of the hall, Jake whistled.

"What are you doing, Birdbrain?" Desmond asked. "Turning into a canary?"

"I wouldn't call me names now, if I were you," Jake replied. "I'm whistling so I can hear the wall."

"Hear the wall?" Desmond sneered. "Is that impossible or what?"

Will this jerk never learn? Jake thought. He was tempted to crash him into the wall. It would serve him right. Still, maybe Desmond was only a little bad, like Wagger at the Birthday. Jake snapped, "Put your left hand out." He kept his own free arm at his side.

"Hey!" Desmond cried. "The wall is right here!" He sounded amazed. "What are you, a magician?"

Jake laughed. "Don't I wish?" They carried on, up the hall and back down. Other pairs of students joined them. Desmond wasn't so bad at listening, when he concentrated. He could tell if kids were behind him or in front of him.

To Jake's surprise, Sir Jake the Handsome and Squire Desmond the Deadbeat reentered the classroom, both of them still upright, neither of them bleeding or bruised.

*****

After dinner, Jake arranged his small bells on the table in a row. He set the alarm on his watch for thirty minutes and stood directly in front of his bells. He'd practice the C Major scale first. It started with good old Chris.

Do re mi, he rang. Keeping a steady rhythm was difficult.

Fa so, the bells pealed. He had to be careful not to move his body sideways, even an inch, or he'd reach too far and pick up Bossy Blake instead of Angel Ann.

La ti do, he rang.

After practicing the scale five times, he decided to try a song. *An easy song*, Mr. O'Shanigan had suggested. The first tune that came to his mind was *Row, Row, Row Your Boat*. Still, he settled on *Are*

You Sleeping? The song was about bells, after all.

It took him forever to figure out the first four notes...Chocolate Chris, Daring Doug, Elephant Emma and then Chocolate Chris again. Once he figured that out, he kept loosing track of the placement of the bells on the table. As hard as he could, Jake concentrated. His watch beeped far too soon. The thirty-minute practice was over.

Time for Math with Mom.

Jake pushed the bells into a clump in the middle of the table. Idly, he picked up one. *Daring Doug,* he thought to himself as he rang it. Then he checked the Braille label. *D,* it said.

Pleased, Jake picked up another bell and shook it. *Golden George*, he decided. It wasn't the sound that he recognized...or at least it wasn't only the sound. No, it was the weight, the feel of the brass bell that he knew by heart. Half in a trance, he checked the label.

G, it said.

Jake grinned. He might not be able to play a song all the way through, but soon he'd be able to design a *fantastic* bell trick.

As the big weekend drew closer, all Jake could think about were the cats in the window well and the Stagecoach Run. At the beginning of his second lesson with Mr. O'Shanigan, he pretended to be riding on a stagecoach as he played his bells. He played along with the imaginary rhythm of the coach rolling across the land.

"Been practicing?" Mr. O'Shanigan asked, offering him a biscuit.

"Yes sir." Jake replied, crunching down, happily surprised that the biscuit ended up being a cookie.

"Your mom's idea, was it?" the bell-ringer asked. "This practicing?"

"Mine," Jake replied.

"Yours, my lad?" Mr. O'Shanigan clapped him on the shoulder, nearly knocking him off his feet. Jake stretched to stand taller. By the end of the lesson they were playing a duet of *Are You Sleeping*. Jake figured it wouldn't be long before they would be playing it as a round.

*****

Friday night, Jake dreamed about two kittens running on their back feet with a rope stretched between them. The kittens wore little bandannas. Then his image shifted, and he dreamed about Mama Cat driving a stagecoach. Only, she spoke with a meowy voice that sounded like his *own* mother. Then he realized it was his mother driving with a tail and little pointed, furry ears.

When he awakened, Jake sat bolt upright in bed. "To dream the impossible dream," his mother was singing in the kitchen. Jake's shoulders slumped in relief. His mother hadn't turned into a cat after all. The next line of her song swirled around him, "To run where the brave dare not go."

Jake slid on his socks toward his dresser by the window. The biggest weekend of his life had arrived. He just hoped he would survive. Running three and a half miles in the hot sun with thousands of other runners could be a disaster. His top drawer opened with a squeak. Jake riffled through his pants until he found his favorite, the soft corduroys.

So far, he'd kept the kittens at the School for the Blind a perfect cloak and dagger operation, just like he'd promised the girls. Jake yanked a t-shirt out of the next drawer. But today was the time for the rescue. Today at noon.

How was he supposed to convince his mother to drive him to meet Eva at the School for the Blind if he couldn't tell her about the stowaways in the window well? Jake tugged the shirt over his head. He checked the label to make sure he hadn't put it on backwards. Besides, getting in big trouble was a possibility. Mom might not approve of him sneaking away from the group on Saturdays to pet a cat...especially a strange, scruffy cat.

Sitting on his closet floor, he slipped on his socks from yesterday. His mother liked him to change his socks every day, but they weren't that dirty.

Not even stinky yet.

Ages ago, Mom had given him a choice. Either he could have stylish clothes and have them marked with tiny plastic triangles and rectangles and circles, so he would know what outfits matched...or she could buy his clothes so that everything matched. He'd chosen the easy route. Every shirt and pair of pants matched. Every sweatshirt. All his socks were white.

Slowly, Jake tied his tennis shoes. He wasn't ready to tell Mom about the kittens. *Not yet.* First, he wanted to talk to Eva to find out more about her rescue plan. He'd see her at the shirt decorating party.

A bowl of Cheerios, two lemon drops and a ten-minute drive later, Jake bounded up Katherine's steps. Wind blustered against his back. In fact, it swept him forward. Jake bumped into someone on the step above him, a person with a wisp of a pond smell.

"Got to keep my feet running," Brandon muttered.

"What?" Jake asked, rubbing his nose.

"That's my goal," Brandon said. "Run, run, run, the whole distance! Never stop."

"My goal is to beat you," Shaniqua called, pounding up the stairs behind them.

Clearly, he wasn't the only one psyched up about this race. Jake stepped into the apartment beside Brandon and Shaniqua squeezed in behind. The wind slammed the door shut behind the three of them with a crash. Instantly, a galloping sound rushed straight toward them, *Galump, galump, galump.*

"Brace yourself!" Brandon exclaimed.

Shaniqua groaned. "Oooo Mama."

Something wet slurped Jake's hand. A long tongue washed his cheek. "Socks!" he cried. If the dog was loose, that meant he wasn't wearing his harness. Socks was fair game for strokes! Jake dropped to his knees and hugged the big guy. He was furry and wiggly and too huge to hold. In other words, he was perfect.

Socks tugged loose and bounded away. Jake sat on the floor and slipped off one of his socks. "Catch," he cried, tossing the sock into the air like a Frisbee.

Snap! Teeth clicked together. Paws scraped the carpet in front of him. *Scritch, scratch, slide!* The dog dashed around behind him.

"What in the world?" Katherine exclaimed from the kitchen.

"Socks?" Jake said as the wind of the dog pummeled in front of him again. *Galump, galump, galump.* The fool dog must be running in circles.

"Here, Socks!" he called again. This hadn't gone quite the way he'd expected. Jake stood up. "I threw the dog my sock," he admitted to Katherine.

The Golden Retriever barked ecstatically and circled Jake again, *Woof, woof, woof!*

"You'll be lucky if you ever wear the sock again." Katherine's laugh filled the room. "That dog nibbles socks. Dirty ones are especially tasty."

Oops, Jake thought. His sock probably did smell dirty to Socks. Dogs could smell lots better than boys. The guide dog slid to a stop in front of him, panting.

Jake spread his arms wide and tiptoed toward the four-legged beast. "Jake, the Dog-nabber, strikes again!" he yelled and leaped.

Socks poked his leg with something soft, most likely his nose. Jake grabbed. To his surprise, only the dog's feathery tail ran through his fingers. Socks had changed direction in midair! Talk about a good trick.

Maybe he should try ignoring the big lug.

Jake squeezed in between Katherine and Brandon at the table. Hopefully, his mother wouldn't be too upset when he returned home with only one sock. The dog plopped down in the corner behind him, snuffling and slurping. Now and then, Socks snapped as if he were throwing the sock in the air and catching it between his teeth.

To Jake's right, Brandon kept clicking his fingers and saying, "*Ne*-ver stop. *Ne*-ver stop."

A snack on the table smelled delicious. With any luck, Katherine had been baking. The Boss made great brownies. Jake sniffed again. Whatever it was didn't smell like chocolate.

"I've been working on a cheer," Shaniqua said from across the table.

"Tell us," Katherine encouraged.

"No way," Shaniqua replied. "It's a secret for tomorrow."

Jake explored the table with his hands. Everybody was acting like nervous cats, as if the fur on the back of their necks was standing straight up. That thought reminded him of Eva. He sure hoped she would arrive soon.

A big pile of puffy round blobs, each about a third the size of a dime, rested in the middle of the table. Little bottles, too. Jake picked up a bottle and squeezed goo onto his finger. Sticky goo. Next, he found tiny stars that stuck to his finger. And hearts.

Finally, his scanning hand touched a platter of warm, sticky bars. Jake plucked one off the plate and held it up to his nose. "Rice crispy treats." Gleefully, he popped an entire square into his mouth. They tasted better that way, all in one bite.

"Each shirts say *Runner Reads Braille* in print on the back, so put your decorations on the front," The Boss said. "Jake, here's a size small for you."

Jake opened his mouth to say thanks. His teeth were stuck together so he murmured, "Ank oo." He located the label on his shirt and stretched it out at his spot, front side up. *Now, I need a design,* he mused.

First, he glued on puffy dots to make his name in Braille. He was surrounding his name with stars when Socks nuzzled him. As Jake patted the dog's head with a sticky hand, the dog whined and plunked a blob onto his knee.

A very soggy blob.

Why, the dog had brought his sock back to him. "Good boy!" The sock was so wet Jake could wring out dog slobber. Still, it only had one little hole in the toe. He scratched Socks' ear.

When Jake's mom picked him up, his right foot made a squelching sound with every step. Worse than that, Eva still hadn't arrived. Jake handed his mother his new shirt.

"Let's see," she said. "What does this say? J...A..." She was usually good at reading Braille.

"K...E. Jake," she finished as they tromped down the stairs. "I like the stars." Then she sang, "*When you wish upon a star.*" As she opened the car door, she said in an aside, "From the Disney movie Pinocchio. Won an Academy Award for Best Song."

Jake knew he couldn't put off telling his mother his secret any longer. *Not one minute.* No matter how she reacted. It was almost noon.

Mom belted out the next line in her soaring soprano, "Makes no difference who you are."

"Uh, Mom," he interrupted. *Squelch* went his right shoe as he climbed inside the van.

He needed her help...

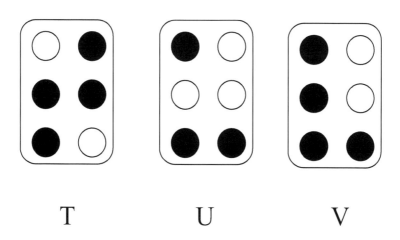

T   U   V

When you are out in public, start noticing where you see Braille. For a start, check out elevators.

13
The Surprise

Mom didn't hum a single note all the way to the School for the Blind. That was a *bad* sign. "You want to save kittens?" she kept exclaiming. *"What do you intend to do with these kittens?"*

"Eva has a plan," Jake replied, tugging on a dry, crusty sock he'd found stuffed into the back seat. At least he hoped she had a plan. "I *promised* I'd help her." Mom was big on promises. The car slanted steeply upward as he double-knotted his laces.

Mom cut right and jerked to a stop. "We're here," she muttered, as grumpy as a bear. "So are Eva and her mother."

"That mama cat is a darling," Eva's mother said in her soft Hispanic accent as Jake yanked open his door. "She walked right up to me. I think we can safely let Evita and little Jake manage alone."

"Gracias, Mama," Eva breathed.

Jake didn't like being called Little Jake. Still, this wasn't the time to argue. Circling the front of the car, he headed straight toward Eva's voice. His hair blew off his forehead. "Hey, Wombat." He slid his hand behind her elbow.

"Hi, Jake the Jester. Knew you'd come."

His mother humphed, but she didn't follow them as they headed off along the sidewalk. Eva could see shadows, and he had his cane, so they made a good pair. The buildings on either side echoed their footsteps. Behind them, he could hear Eva's mom speaking, "I agreed she could keep the mama cat. My Evita has a soft heart for cats. Besides, when you take a kitten, we'll only need to find a home for one."

Above the whine of the wind, Jake heard his mother choke. As Eva veered left, his cane slid off the sidewalk onto the soft grass. In a few steps, the grown-ups' voices vanished. Jake tugged on his friend's arm. "Why did you tell your mother I'm going to take a kitten?"

"Oh Jake, I'm sorry." Eva carried something bulky that bumped into his leg. "Would *you* rather keep the mama cat?"

Jake didn't know what to say. "No, no." They would figure it all out later. He couldn't imagine what his mother might be thinking right now.

He whistled. The back of the building rose beside them. *Close by.* He rolled the tip of his cane from side to side, mostly to his left. He didn't want to tumble into the window well by accident.

Meow.

Jake froze and held his breath. To his delight, he heard several cries, most of them little. *Mew. Mew. Mew.* The cats had survived raccoons, groundskeeper and guide dogs! The mother cat yowled again, closer, and then rubbed against his ankles. Jake dropped to the ground and stroked her soft fur. "You big, brave cat. " A burst of wind flattened her fur.

"Here's the cat carrier," Eva said.

Running his fingertips over the box, Jake found windows on each side covered with mesh, so a cat inside the cage could breath, but not escape. It had a handle on top, too. He wiggled a little finger through the bars on the front door and then unlatched it.

"I've got sliced turkey," Eva said. He helped her place the snack inside the carrier in the back. Before they could pull their hands out, the mother cat stuck her head in.

"Stardust," Eva crooned. Meredith had said that the mother cat had a star on her chest.

It's a good name, Jake thought, tugging his hand free.

"Push her!" Eva cried. They both shoved the cat on the rump. With a muffled squeak, Stardust slid into the carrier. Instantly, Jake could hear her gobbling.

"Quick." Eva latched the door. "Let's get the babies, while she's busy."

When Jake lay down on his belly by the window well, the kittens greeted him with tiny meows. They must not be big enough to jump out yet. They were protected from the wind down there, too.

"Tst, tst, tst," Eva clicked in Catlish beside him. "Hi, pretty babies." She switched to Spanish, "Hola, babés bonitísimos."

With a yelp, she flinched, "Ouch! It scratched me!" Jake could hear her sucking her finger. "Gone wild," she muttered.

Taking a deep breath, Jake slipped his own hand down into the window well. The kittens weren't wild. They just hadn't seen people in a month. He didn't try to feel for one of the kittens. Instead, he let his fingers dangle. Sure enough, one of the cats wandered over to investigate. He could feel the fur.

"Meoow," the mother cat sang out. She must have *already* finished eating the turkey. A tiny nose tickled Jake's finger. He didn't see how he could hurry. He stroked the kitten with one finger, moving as slowly as a caterpillar. He even stroked the tail, the bent tail.

This was Squirt, the littlest one!

"Mew," said Squirt. The sound caught at Jake's heart. It was such a baby.

"Meoooooowwwwww!" yowled the mother.

He'd always yearned for a dog. A big dog. The bigger the better. Still, this kitten felt soft and gentle. It couldn't help not being born a dog. With a quick swoop, Jake slid his hand underneath its belly and lifted. "Got you!" Squirt didn't even struggle.

Good kitty, Jake thought.

Once he'd lifted him out of the well, Squirt spit, "Pst pst pst."

"Meoww ft ft fttttt!" answered the mother, clearly furious at being a prisoner.

Squirt wiggled wildly in Jake's hand. One tiny paw swiped his thumb. It stung like a bee sting, a fiery wasp sting! Not knowing what else to do, Jake dropped the little guy into the bottom of his shirt and rolled him up.

"I'll get the other one." Eva crooned, "Come here, feisty one."

A singsong growling rose from the window well. The hair on the back of Jake's neck rose. How could one little kitten make *that* noise? The mother cat set up an even louder racket on the other side of him.

"Unlock the carrier," Eva begged.

When Jake touched the carrier door, a paw reached through the open bars and wrapped around his finger. A very strong paw.

"Stop that!" Jake ordered, thumping the side of the carrier with his foot. Luckily, the mother cat let go. Holding the carrier motionless between his feet, he clasped the hissing kitten tightly in his shirt and fumbled at the latch with his free hand.

"Ha, I've got this one by the back of the neck," Eva said triumphantly.

Somehow, Jake unlocked the carrier door without dropping the kitten. The mother cat's yowling grew even louder, "MEOOOWW. Fttttt. GRRRRRrrr."

He felt Eva's hand on his.

"Now!" she exclaimed over the awful screeching. Jake wrenched open the carrier. Eva shoved her kitten inside. Together, they slammed the door, and Eva latched it. Instantly, Stardust stopped howling.

"Good cat," Eva said weakly.

Careful not to drop or squish the baby wrapped in his shirt, Jake stood. A gust of wind swirled around him, so strong that he wobbled back onto his heels.

"Pst," the little guy hissed. Then he added more plaintively, "Mew."

"You're safe," Jake replied, leaning his head down close to reassure him. He felt the kitten lurch in his shirt. Then he felt the wind of a tiny paw slicing the air near his nose.

Jake jerked his head out of range.

Tucking his cane under his arm, he reached down to hold Eva's elbow. She stooped to pick up the carrier. Together, they turned so the wind was at their backs and made their way, very slowly, to the cars.

Eva's mother oohed and aahed, but his mother remained silent.

"Guess, I'd better give you this kitten, too," Jake muttered. Taking a chance of his finger being sliced, he stroked the soft fur of the silent kitten, then the tiny bent tail. To his surprise, his throat thickened with tears. "Mom?"

And his mother was there, her arm around him. "Seems like a nice kitten," she said, drawing him behind the car, out of the wind. "It likes you."

"His name's Squirt," Jake said. "Or hers."

"You named it?" Mom sounded astonished.

"Ages ago," Jake admitted. He could hear Eva and her mother talking about Stardust in rapid Spanish. He couldn't stop himself, he begged, "Mom, I know you said I was too young for a pet, but..."

"I said you were too young for a dog, Jake," she

interrupted. "All you've ever wanted is a *huge* dog. I never said a word about a cat." Mom hesitated.

Jake waited, holding his breath.

"I thought a cat might...well...disturb you," Mom said. "Cats pounce on people without making a sound. They don't give any warning. And they play with anything that moves, like a cane."

Jake leaned against his mother. "I've got pretty good ears." He stroked the kitten with one finger. To Jake's astonishment, Squirt purred. "Hear that?"

Mom laughed. "No, but I can see its little body rumbling." She made a considering sort of sound. "You're old enough to start making your own choices, Jake. And to start living with the consequences."

Jake leaned back, enjoying his mother's softness.

"I must say you are doing pretty well so far," she added.

So far? he wondered.

Her arm tightened around him. "You'll have to take good care of your new pet, son."

Jake gasped, hugging Squirt so close that the little guy squeaked. "Let's go home! All three of us!"

"Hasta luego, amigo," Eva called as he bounded into the car.

"Bye, Wombat!" he answered. Carefully, Jake cradled the baby that was hardly bigger than his hand. He repeated Mom's words in his mind. Never in a million years had he thought he would ever hear his mother say those words.

Your new pet...

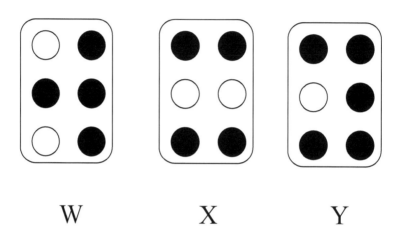

W X Y

For a sighted person, learning Braille feels like you are learning a new language. What you are really learning is a new way to read and write the language you already know.

14
Applesauce Cake

All afternoon, Squirt rode around inside Jake's shirt. The furry body felt warm and ticklish against his stomach. Half the time the kitten slept. The rest of the time, he purred. When Mom fried turkey burgers, Squirt stuck his head out between two buttons on Jake's shirt, mewing.

"Hungry?" Jake knelt on the floor and shook dried cat food onto a plate. He kept two gentle fingers on the cat. Instead of eating, Squirt arched his back and skittered away. The little guy sounded like a bicycle tire loosing air in spurts. "Ft, ftt, ftttt."

Jake crawled under the table after him. "You don't know it yet, fierce guy," he crooned, "but you've won the cat lottery living here. Good eats. Great tricks." Scooping up the kitten, Jake slid out from under the table on his knees. Next, he poured milk into a bowl.

Squirt wouldn't drink either.

"You'll starve if you don't eat!" Jake exclaimed and pushed the kitten's nose into the milk. Squirt sneezed. At least Jake thought it was a sneeze. Then Squirt climbed right into the bowl. The little kitten lapped and slurped and sneezed.

When his stomach bulged, Jake lifted him out of the milk and carried him to the sink. He wiped his milky legs off with a damp paper towel. "Stop squirming, Squirt." Less than a minute later, the kitten fell asleep inside his shirt.

That evening, Mom baked an applesauce cake. It was a tradition in their family for important occasions. Mom said it would help him run better, all those carbohydrates. She mixed in tons of raisins and then iced the cake with a cream cheese frosting. "I'm proud of you for choosing to stick with the running," she said, as she set the first slice down in front of him. "Very proud, Jake."

The aroma of cinnamon and ginger wafted toward his nose. Jake's toes wiggled when the first warm bite of applesauce cake melted in his mouth. As he was nibbling on his third piece, Dad called. They talked about *Redwall* and Squirt and the Stagecoach Run.

"Run hard, Champ," Dad said before he hung up. "I'll be thinking about you tomorrow.

When Jake climbed into bed, Squirt purred on his chest. He knew he would always think of this cat as his tenth birthday present, even if he had arrived four weeks early. The kitten scooted forward and pressed his tiny head under Jake's chin.

This was the time of night he always created a

Flying Wagger story. Jake imagined Bert and the guide dog and Squirt together. Maybe Squirt could ride on the dog's harness – the feisty feline, swiping at danger with his tiny paw.

Jake stroked him with one finger. He was such a little guy. Babies needed lots of help to grow up. "Don't worry," Jake said. "I'll help you figure out the important stuff, like the milk." He yawned. "First, I'll show you how not to make Mom mad."

Jake tugged gently on an itsy bitsy ear. "And how to avoid being chased by dogs." The kitten purred louder. "How to act fierce. It's all in noticing what's important, really. Paying attention. Like in my tricks."

The raisins and cream cheese in Jake's stomach gurgled. "If I survive the race, I'll teach you. I promise." At that thought, the three slices of cake in his stomach turned a flip. When he awakened, it would be time for *The Stagecoach Run.* He hadn't felt so nervous since the first day of school when he'd learned that Ms. Rose was the strictest teacher in Ellington Elementary.

As his head sank to one side on his pillow, he imagined the running monster jogging around his bed. "Tomorrow's the day," the running monster was singing, off key. "Tomorrow's the day."

His imagination was sure full of vim and vigor tonight. That was one of Dad's sayings. Jake rolled over and patted the top of his nightstand to find Meredith's good luck charm. He slipped the bracelet on. Then he rested his head on St. Bernie and drifted asleep.

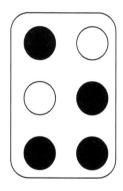

Z

Congratulations! Now you know the entire alphabet in Braille. Bake an applesauce cake with your favorite adult. It's time to celebrate!

15
Runner Reads Braille

M om shook him awake so early the sparrows weren't even chirping. Shivering, Jake pulled on his *Runner Reads Braille* shirt. All the Roadrunners would be wearing them, volunteers, too. With a yawn, he slipped on his sweatpants, knotted his tennis shoes, and padded into the kitchen with a sleepy Squirt cradled in one arm.

He managed to swallow three bites of oatmeal. Then he shut the kitten in the pantry. No matter what happened at the Stagecoach Run, Squirt would be waiting for him when he returned.

Mew, Squirt howled. *Mew*.

They drove in silence. The smell of Mom's coffee filled the car. After awhile, the van halted. "Here we are, Jake." She didn't turn off the engine. "I'm going to park near the finish line, so I can cheer for you."

He wanted to yell, *No, no! Don't leave me!*

Instead, he opened the car door. Whistles blew as policemen directed traffic. The air felt moist and cool. Familiar voices tumbled over each other a few feet away. Jake unfolded his cane and stepped into the parking lot. "Bye, Mom."

"Good luck, Babe," she said. She hadn't called him *Babe* in ages. As the car pulled away, Jake stood still, listening to the shouted greetings of thousands of people.

Brakes squeaked. Horns blared. Doors slammed.

"Hey Jake!" The Boss called. It was good to hear her voice. "Come get your number."

Sliding the tip of his cane from side to side, Jake headed toward his group. Katherine handed him a paper that seemed to be in the shape of a circle...with spokes. "A wheel?" Jake asked.

"You and Meredith are in the *Wheel Group*," The Boss explained, "along with Eva and Mr. Solomon, because you expect to run part of the way and walk part of the way." Carefully, Jake unhooked the safety pins and pinned it to his shirt.

"I'm a horse!" Brandon exclaimed, letting Jake feel his number. It had four legs and a tail. He and Adam and Shaniqua and Adele were in the *Horse Group* since they planned to run the entire way. Katherine and her partner had been chosen to be in the *Driver Group* because they ran fast.

"Would you *please* stop snorting?" Shaniqua said.

Brandon kept right on neighing. "I'm a horse!" I'm a horse!"

"Enjoying the dawn, Cuz?" Meredith mumbled.

"Shut your mouth, you galloping fool!" Shaniqua snapped.

"Can't do anything with him when he's hyped up." Meredith yawned so widely that Jake could hear her. He reached for her wrist, feeling gently with his fingertips. Sure enough, she wore a bracelet, too.

"Mine's purple and yellow," she said. "For my hair and my favorite color."

Brandon circled off to neigh at someone else.

"You have purple hair?" Jake teased. Suddenly, he felt sorry that he hadn't brought Meredith a good luck charm. They were partners, after all. He could have made her something. An idea popped into his head. Wasn't she thinking about becoming a vision teacher? "Hey Meredith, want to learn Braille?"

"I taught myself the alphabet. But Katherine gave me a Braille book to read, and it didn't make sense," Meredith moaned. "There was a Y symbol right in the middle of a sentence, all by itself."

Jake couldn't resist laughing. "Stands for you."

"What?" Meredith said.

"The alphabet is Grade One Braille." Jake jiggled from foot to foot in the cold. "Most books are written in Grade Two Braille. Letters alone stand for words. B stands for but. C stands for can." Jake started to sing the ABC song, "A, but, can, do, every, from, go."

"I don't get it," Meredith moaned.

"So, I'll teach you," Jake declared. "I'm a champ at reading Braille." He didn't tell her about the one hundred and eighty-six contractions, like st and ch.

"How's Squirt?" Eva interrupted.

Jake felt good standing shoulder to shoulder with Eva. Well, shoulder to elbow. He remembered what Eva had said yesterday as they had driven away from the School for the Blind, "Hasta luego, amigo." He knew *hasta luego* meant *see you later*. But the important word had been the last one. Amigo. *Friend.*

Meredith wanted to hear every detail of their adventure, from setting off alone around the building, to shoving the mama cat into the carrier, to snagging the kittens out of the window well. When they finished the story, she sighed, "Stardust and Squirt. Let's see, the other kitten has a white tip on its tail and a white face, but its body is black." Meredith giggled. "How about calling it Sandwich? Then we'd have Stardust, Squirt, and Sandwich."

A moment later, she murmured, "Do you think? Maybe?"

Jake wondered what she was talking about.

Meredith added, "I'd *have* to ask my dad."

"It would be perfect," Eva cried. Both girls screeched, their voices bouncing up and down like rubber balls. Why, Meredith wanted the other kitten! When the girls grabbed Jake's arms, he danced a few steps, too.

"What would be perfect?" Brandon asked.

So Mere *had* kept the kittens a complete secret, even from her own cousin. Just as she'd promised. Jake found he wasn't surprised. Not one bit.

"Dragon Breath," Brandon insisted.

"He only calls me that when I drive him nuts," Meredith whispered in Jake's ear.

"After the race, I'm going to go home and write a new song," Eva announced.

The three secret-keepers chorused, "The Cat Who Lived at the School for the Blind." Next, they repeated the story for Brandon and Shaniqua from start to finish. After all, the kittens didn't need to be kept top secret any longer.

"Humph," Shaniqua grumbled, and Jake knew she wished she could have been part of the adventure, too.

"Baby animals growing up in the window well," Brandon murmured. "While *we* practiced."

In the windy dawn, the Roadrunners formed their circle. Jake stood between Meredith and Brandon. On important days, the group stood still for a minute of silence. Jake imagined holding his arms out wide and giving the earth a hug.

During stretching, he crossed his feet and touched his toes. Then he wobbled. *Oops,* Jake thought, trying to catch his balance. Suddenly, he and Brandon leaned into each other like lopsided teepees.

"Slip and slide time, Dude," Brandon said.

As the early morning chill crept up his legs, Shaniqua taught them her cheer,

"We're the Roadrunners, yes we *a-are*,
We're the Roadrunners, we'll go *fa-ar*,
Here we come, two by *two-oo*,
Better watch out...or we'll PASS YOU!"

Everyone whistled and cheered. They chanted the words, clapping. "Louder," Shaniqua boomed in her deepest voice. "I can't hear you!" Everyone roared the cheer again.

Then it was Katherine's turn. "Good luck, Roadrunners," The Boss said warmly. "Remember, there will be water at two miles. I'll be waiting for each and every one of you at the end. Unless you beat *me* to the finish line." She laughed, fired up. "After we're all finished, we'll head to the stage. A television reporter called me last night. She wants to interview us. Adventure Sports will be on the evening news."

Excellent, Jake thought. When the reporter asked him why he was running, he'd say, *I want to raise money for my old kindergarten.* That would sound better than telling the whole world that his goal was to make it to the finish line.

The Boss clapped her hands three times. "Move to your starting positions! Guides, look for the wheel signs and horse signs along the side of the road."

Jake gripped Meredith's elbow as they slipped into the crowd. People brushed against him. He stayed silent and let Meredith and Mr. Solomon figure out where they should be. So did Eva. Soon they came to a standstill, jostling a bit of space so the four of them could stand side by side. High voices and low voices surrounded them...men, women, children.

"Welcome to the ninth annual Stagecoach Run," an announcer boomed. "Our youngest runner today is five years old and our oldest is ninety-two. Eight thousand of us have raised eighty thousand dollars for Branstock, our Kindergarten for the Visually Impaired. I want to offer a very special welcome to the graduates of Branstock who are running this morning. Visually impaired runners will be dressed in bright orange T-shirts."

His voice softened, "In a few moments, our race will begin. Drivers will lead off. Six minutes later, the Horses will start. Six minutes after that, the Wheels. Finally, the Walkers." He cleared his throat. "I've been asked to remind you there will be no running baby strollers. All baby strollers must walk."

"Can baby strollers walk?" Meredith mused.

Mr. Solomon chuckled. "Beats me."

"Good luck, Drivers," the announcer yelled. A giant bell clanged, and the race began. Thousands upon thousands of voices rose together into a shout. The hair on the back of Jake's neck stood straight up.

Minutes later, the bell rang again and the Horses were off. "Go, Brandon," he and Meredith shouted.

"Run, Shaniqua!" Eva and Mr. Solomon yelled.

Jake felt as if he was breathing in bubbly energy instead of air. He wanted to sit down and think about it, but he didn't have time. The Wheels would be next.

"Jake," a familiar voice called.

He turned his head toward her. It was Emily. She must be standing on the sidelines. "Hey, Emily!"

"Knock 'em dead, Jake!" she screeched.

"I have a new kitten named Squirt," he yelled.

Like a distant wisp of sound, Jake thought he heard Ms. Rose's soft voice trumpeting, "Good luck, Jake." That had to be his imagination, didn't it? What would his teacher be doing here, cheering him on? He wasn't bored out of his mind in math anymore or the weakest in his class. Actually, he was working his way up to being in the middle group.

It was his coin trick that had given him the answer. He focused in math the same way he listened during his tricks, the way he paid attention when he dropped coins or when was trying to develop a bell trick...with his mind and his ears and even his body.

"Blast off time," Meredith said, interrupting his thoughts. She handed him his end of the skinny little piece of rope. Reluctantly, he let go of her elbow.

"Buena suerte, Jake the Jester," Eva said, barely loudly enough to hear. "You too, Meredith."

Jake opened his mouth to answer, but no sound emerged. Not even a squeak.

"Run hard, Wheels!" the announcer boomed.

The giant bell clanged. Jake could hear the thumping of the footsteps, thousands of footsteps. *Tromp, tromp.* People were packed in around him. He'd never been this close to so many people in his life. Everyone was thrilled, like at an amusement park.

Tromp, tromp. Tromp, tromp.

"Good luck, children," Mr. Solomon said.

Jake gripped his end of the rope. No running monster was going to bother him today. He was so pumped up that he ran and ran. People along the sidelines cheered, and strangers wished him luck. It felt like a giant party. Too bad there wasn't confetti.

"Go!" "Marco!" "Polo!" three voices called, the littlest one last. It was Jared, Jeremy and John. Jake waved wildly. He ran on and on, forever.

"One mile," Meredith announced.

"One?" Jake gasped. "That's all!" He couldn't believe it. He still had over two miles to go? *Maybe I shouldn't bother lifting my feet so high,* he thought.

"Hey, don't slow down," his partner said. "You're doing great." He kept running, though his chest felt as if it might burst.

"Ooops." Meredith's voice shot up, "Careful. There's a dip in..."

That's when the toe of his left tennis shoe caught in a hole. Or maybe the running monster tripped him with one of his size twenty-six shoes. Jake was going so fast that he didn't stumble. *No,* he sailed forward, into nothingness. "Aaahh," he yelled.

The rope ripped out of his hand.

He was airborne. Not a single part of his body touched the earth. It was as if time froze, and he hung in the air. Jake's right elbow hit first and scraped along the asphalt. He slid on his hands, too, somehow managing to keep his face off the ground.

When he skidded to a stop, Jake rolled into a ball, hugging his stinging elbow to his chest and breathing so hard that he sounded as if he were crying. Stickiness bathed his elbow, and his right hand burned like fire. Then he really did start to cry.

"Stand up, Jake!" Meredith ordered. "You don't want to get trampled, do you?" With sudden strength, she hauled him to his feet.

His head swirled, so he leaned against her.

"The palm of your hand is the worst," she moaned. He could hear the tears in her voice, too. "Oh Jake, are you all right?"

"I want to quit," Jake screamed, so loudly that his voice cracked. "NOW!"

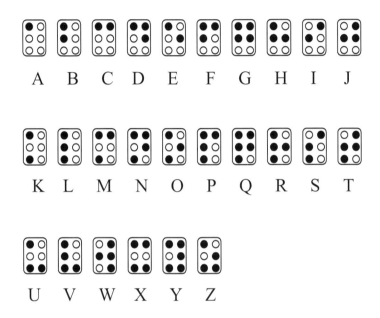

Above, is the entire alphabet in Braille. Try writing a note to a friend! Or wow your mom with your new knowledge.

16
A Skinny Little Piece of Rope

W here are all the grownups when you need them?" Meredith moaned. "Katherine, Mr. Solomon, Adele," her voice rose. "Not a one of them in sight!" With a whimper, Jake stomped his feet on the pavement. The salty odor of his own blood filled his nostrils. Tromping footsteps divided and pounded around them in two streams.

Meredith patted his good arm. She took a deep, shaky breath. "Clamp your hand into a fist to stop the bleeding." The older girl showed Jake how to curl his fingers tight. "*Now*, let's walk! Katherine said there'd be water at two miles. Adults will help us there."

"I've got blood dripping down my arm!" Jake objected. "And you want to keep going?"

"We don't have a choice," Meredith snapped, as if she were a drill sergeant. She slipped that stupid little piece of rope into his good hand. "Let's go!"

A volcano inside his chest began erupting in spurts of hot lava. He strode along, murmuring, "Slave driver. Drill sergeant. Fat lot of good a lucky bracelet did me." He held his right arm close to his body instead of swinging it.

Sure enough, at the water station, when Meredith said, "My partner fell and..."

Two people interrupted in one hearty breath, "We'll clean you right up, young man!"

Jake shrank a step away.

"Here's hydrogen peroxide." A woman grasped his upper arm in a wrestler's grip. "Hold still now."

"Won't hurt a bit." The man clasped his wrist.

Meredith squeezed his free hand. Jake had to admit it felt nice.

"Ready?" the man asked. Before Jake could open his mouth to answer, something wet dribbled over his elbow. It stung like a hundred wasps.

"Yeow!" Jake exclaimed, but the man kept right on pouring. Jake struggled to pull free, but the woman held him as firmly as a wet dog in a bathtub. Jake gave up fighting in a daze of stinging. They bound his elbow around and around with gauze. Next, both adults scrubbed at his palm and stuck on a giant Band-Aid, wrapping tape around that, too. He felt like a policeman injured in the line of duty.

Meredith led him aside where it was quieter, and the smell of pine needles surrounded them. "What do you say now?" she asked.

Jake took a deep breath. His mind was screaming, *Don't be a fool! Save your life! Jump ship!*

But his worst fear had already happened.

If he quit, he might not do the Stagecoach Run next year. He might not try to run when he was big enough to be a Horse, like Brandon. He could tell Meredith was holding her breath, waiting for his answer. The last of his anger vanished. It wasn't Mere's fault he'd fallen. She'd been frightened, too.

The Boss would be waiting for him at the end. Not to mention his mother and twenty thousand other people. Jake sighed. Hadn't he been determined to prove that he wasn't a scared sort of boy?

The problem was...

Jake shivered, goose bumps growing on his arms. The image of the running monster rose in his mind. Maybe the ogre was waiting for him on the second half of the run.

No way, he thought. The running monster wasn't hiding out there somewhere. The monster in tennis shoes was sticking *close* to him. *Very close.* As a matter of fact, he could imagine the creature sitting on his shoulder, dangling his enormous feet against his chest. Jake swallowed. His daydreaming was getting the better of him. Still, he might as well admit it.

He *was* frightened. No, he was scared out of his socks. Jake took a deep breath, listening to runners racing past on the nearby pavement and the volunteers offering water.

Jake spun his good luck charm on his wrist. Even if he was scared, his feet could still run. *Right?* His lungs could still breathe. One of his hands could still grip that rope.

Being afraid didn't mean he couldn't keep going.

"I'll...try," Jake muttered.

Meredith squealed and hugged him so hard she nearly cracked his ribs. That squeeze started him running down the road. He'd never been hugged by a teenage girl before.

Soon, his tennis shoes scraped along the asphalt. He sounded like a hippopotamus, not a roadrunner. Jake tried to jog, but he couldn't lift his sneakers. They weighed a ton. He leaned back against the rope.

He even thought he heard Desmond cheering. That had to be a fantasy. The two of them might not be *push-him-off-a-cliff* enemies anymore, but they sure weren't friends.

"We're almost finished," Meredith kept on saying.

He didn't believe her. He clutched the skinny, little piece of rope. His world narrowed to lifting his feet...and his aching palm.

Throb, throb, throb, moaned his elbow.

Meredith dragged him along. Running power wouldn't keep him going, that was for sure. Jake imagined Flying Wagger sailing out in front of him. Tiny wings on the dog's feet fluttered a million miles an hour. The dog wore a cape that said *Willpower* in Braille.

Jake sighed. He liked tricks, didn't he? Well, it was time to try a new one. His daydreaming was like a coin. A two sided coin. On one side was the running monster, sitting on his shoulder. On the other side was good old Flying Wagger, soaring in front of him. His imagination could either scare the socks off him...or help him get this race finished.

He took one step. Or maybe it was a hundred.

Jake imagined himself wearing a *willpower* cape, just like the flying guide dog. A magician's cape. Flying Wagger skyrocketed in front of him, hovering above the crowd, wagging his tail wildly. All the people sitting in lawn chairs along the road cheered.

And he kept on moving.

Two more steps. Or maybe it was two hundred.

He imagined prying the running monster off his shoulder and setting him on the ground. *Snort, snort, snort*, objected the creature out of his three noses. Jake shoved the monster on the back to get him running. As the humongous feet vanished into the crowd, he waved goodbye.

Then he concentrated on Flying Wagger drawing him forward. On *willpower.* Jake lifted his head, imagining the dog with his mind's eye. He focused with his heart, with his brain, with every bit of himself.

And he kept on moving.

Three more steps. Or maybe it was three hundred.

He heard a band playing music. He even recognized the song, *She'll be Coming Round the Mountain.* Jake straightened his back. He really was almost at the finish line. Then he heard a familiar voice. "Here comes Jake," Mr. Solomon shouted.

"Come on, Whistling Boy!" Shaniqua cried. "Move those feet."

"Look at that Dude run," Brandon hollered. And Jake did start to run.

"Go!" Eva screeched. "You are looking so good."

Suddenly, he heard the *tromp-tromp tromp-tromp* of footsteps falling in around him. His friends were running with him toward the finish line. Brandon, Eva, even Shaniqua!

He was one of the Roadrunners. He was a member of a team. For the first time in his life. And he was running. Really running. Jake lifted his feet and leaned forward. He could feel the wind on his face and hear the roaring of thousands of voices.

Katherine's voice boomed over the loudspeaker, "Here comes Jake Howard, a nine-year-old from Ellington Elementary, a first time runner. We're proud of you, Jake."

The Boss had announced his name! Jake couldn't believe it. That's what she'd meant when she said she would be waiting for each and every one of them at the end. He stretched his legs and sprinted faster.

For The Boss.

For the team.

For himself.

Being the youngest of all didn't matter. Not one bit. Eva ran on his right side with Mr. Solomon. Brandon ran on his left next to Meredith. Shaniqua and Adele pounded along behind. All of them cheered. He didn't need to be taller or stronger or faster or even handsome. His friends liked him just the way he was. Pumping his legs, Jake rocketed toward the end.

Trumpets blared and electric guitars twanged. His heart throbbed, *Boom-BOOM, Boom-BOOM!* Jake imagined Wagger hovering in mid-air above the finish line, taking a bow in his Willpower cape. Thousands of voices cheered for the flying guide dog.

"Hurray for Wagger!" Jake yelled at the top of his lungs. He crossed the finish line. Jake stumbled to a stop. He leaned over and put his hands on his knees, gasping in air. Instantly, his mother was there, hugging him and oohing over his arm.

Meredith thumped him on the back. "Good job, partner!" Then she panted in a puzzled voice, "'Hurray for waffles?'"

"Wagger," Jake managed to wheeze.

Meredith sucked in air, then whomped him so enthusiastically she almost knocked him over. "After you teach me Braille, we should write a story about Flying Wagger. In Braille! We both like reading, don't we? Why not try writing?"

Jake groaned. Writing a book would be worse than running three miles. It would be *impossible*. "Nothing doing!" he spluttered. Then he remembered that he'd said those exact words to his mother when they were sitting at the kitchen table the first time he'd heard about the Stagecoach Run.

And look at him now.

The Adventure Sports gang surrounded him. Jake stood up straight and pumped his good hand into the air like the leader of a parade. Together, they began to sing, "We're the Roadrunners, yes we a-re, We're the Roadrunners, we'll go fa-ar..."

"I did it! I did it! I did it!" Jake yelled.

- *Soften vanilla ice cream. Leave it out of the refrigerator for half an hour.*

- *Mix in Jellybeans. Scoop the ice cream into a big bowl, mix in a giant bag of your favorite jellybeans, and stir and stir and stir.*

- *Refreeze the ice cream. Cover the bowl and put it back in the freezer for a couple of hours.*

- *Serve your homemade treat!*

17
Jellybean Ice Cream

Poised in stillness, Jake stood in front of a table beside Eva's keyboard. His white-gloved hands rested on the first two bells he had to play. As the people in his backyard drifted into silence, he heard sparrows chirping and wind sighing in the trees. Mr. O'Shanigan had loaned him the fancy bells for his party. Best of all, Mom had given him a year of handbell lessons for his tenth birthday.

"One, two, three, four," Eva whispered, as she had so many times before.

It was hard to ring a bell, put it down and wrap his fingers around the next one – all while playing with his other hand. Over and over during the last month, he'd had to remind himself that a boy who could run three miles could do anything.

Remember, Sir Boy, Jake thought as he lifted the first bell high with a swooping glide.

Eva began, playing her keyboard and singing the song they had created together to the tune of *Over the River and Through the Woods*,

"Round the tra-ack and up the hill,
To the window-well we go."

Jake played the accents, *Ding-ding, dong.*

"Looking for that, mysterious cat,
To find babies all in a row-ow," Eva sang.

Here was where it became tricky. Ringing the accents was hard enough. Now he had to sing and play the melody. One mistake and he would be off the beat all the way through. Taking a deep breath, Jake joined Eva, trying to make their voices sound like one,

"Pockets of burritos and gummy worms
We sneak, we tread, we glide,
To feed our friends, our stowaways,
At the famous School of the Blind."

Parents in the audience started chuckling. They'd never heard the song before. The second time through, the Adventure Sports gang joined in singing, just as they'd practiced. Jake relaxed and missed a note.

"Bravo!" parents yelled, clapping.

"Yippee!" hollered the youngsters, stomping their feet. Adventure Sports kids loved to cheer.

Eva touched his arm, and they bowed, side by side. Jake held up a white-gloved hand for silence, the way Mom had taught him. He was a jester, a player of tricks. To his surprise, this one worked. "Dessert," he announced. "Please join us for Jellybean Ice Cream."

"Jake's very own invention," Mom called from the table set up outside the kitchen door.

As Jake grabbed his cane and headed toward his mother's voice, Eva slipped him a bag. Mom had insisted he write *No Presents* on the invitation. Jake reached into the tiny sack and pulled out something soft. It had whiskers and a tail. "A stuffed mouse?"

"Sí. Para Squirt," Eva whispered, "To chase."

"Gracías," Jake whispered back. He helped his mother serve ice cream, handing out bowls forever. Brandon and Emily had at least two bowls each.

As Jake swallowed his first delicious bite of Jellybean Ice Cream, Brandon put a square box into his hands that had holes punched in the top. Jake heard a *thump-thump*. The box had a pondish smell. "Brandon?" he murmured, loosening the lid.

"Aaahh!" Mom yelled, snatching the box away from him. "Not a frog!"

"That's Ms. Hoppy," Brandon objected.

"We'll decide this *later*, Jake," Mom said darkly. She added in a softer tone, "Together."

Jake shifted from foot to foot. His mother hadn't said, "Over my dead body, can you have a frog!" Mom had been acting so strange lately. He picked up his ice cream. First, she'd let him choose all by himself if he wanted to go back to running practice, without hassling.

He slurped a bite. Then she'd let *him* decide if he wanted a kitten as a pet. Jake chewed on a grape jellybean. And there had been the bells – whether or not to practice. She'd left the decision completely up to him. And when he had practiced, she'd given him a year's worth of lessons!

He sucked at a tangerine jellybean. Mom wouldn't have treated him this way a year ago. *No way.* A meowing bundle of fur leaped onto his shoulder.

"Hi, Squirt," Jake said, stroking his furry head. "Feeling brave?" The kitten purred, his best motorboat imitation. "How'd you get out?" The kitten swiped at his hair. *Having a frog would be fun,* Jake thought. Brandon might even visit a lot. But Squirt would adore something that hopped all the time.

Jake sighed. Mom would make him live with his choice; that was for sure. Keeping a bouncy frog and a feisty cat apart in his bedroom would be horrible. He guided the older boy's hand to feel the kitten's claws. Brandon whistled, impressed. "Squirt likes to pounce on anything that moves," Jake said.

"He has sharp teeth?" Brandon growled.

"Mom saw him gobble up a grasshopper in one bite," Jake agreed, and then he added bloodthirstily, "*After* he'd ripped off a leg."

"Where's Ms. Hoppy?" Brandon demanded.

"I'll give your frog back to you when you leave, Brandon," Jake's mother replied. Jake wasn't at all surprised she had stayed near enough to listen. "Until then, I think I'll shut her in a nice safe cupboard." The weight of the kitten vanished from Jake's shoulder. "I'll take this cat, too."

"Meeoowwww," Squirt objected.

Brandon rested his hand on Jake's arm. "Sorry, I can't let you keep Miss Hoppy."

"No problem." Jake wrapped an arm around his friend's shoulder. After a moment, he said, "You must have been terrified in that fire."

Brandon muttered something, but he didn't pull away. Then he said, "Mom thinks I should have an operation this summer on my vocal chords to make my voice normal. The doctor says it might not work."

Jake thumped him on the back. "I'd give a house full of jellybeans to have a voice like yours!"

Brandon stood motionless. "Like mine?"

"Bet you could become a country singer," Jake replied. "Want another bowl of ice cream?"

"Think your Mom would give me a double scoop?" Brandon asked. "Maybe a triple, Dude?"

Everyone ate gallons of Jellybean Ice Cream. Emily, Mr. O'Shanigan, the "J" brothers, Katherine and the Adventure Sports kids played games, ate chips and laughed for hours.

"I've got to go, partner," Meredith finally said. She handed him some papers. "Here's our first Flying Wagger story, typed in Braille by you know who!" It was a story they had made up at the pool. Bert was surfing with Flying Wagger when a dolphin nudged the surfboard. The dolphin led them to an island where Wagger discovered pirates' gold.

Jake ran his fingers over the title. *Flying Wagger's Adventure at the Biach.* He didn't say a word. E and I were mirror opposites of each other in Braille. It was an easy mistake for a beginner.

"Thanks for coming," Jake called from the front steps as the two cousins walked down the path. Squirt sat on his shoulder. "Bye, Brandon."

"Brandon? Did you say Brandon?" His mother

gasped from the living room. A moment later, she raced past Jake down the steps. "Better take your frog home, Brandon."

"Miss Hoppy!" Jake heard his friend say. He sure loved frogs.

One by one, Jake said farewell to his guests. Last of all, he and Shaniqua stood side by side on the porch. The youngest and the oldest.

"How did you make that ice cream?" Shaniqua demanded. Jake whistled mysteriously. She wouldn't have asked if she hadn't liked the way it tasted.

"Another secret?" Shaniqua asked, leaning closer. "Like those gummy worms."

"A real cloak and dagger operation," Jake replied. There was no way she could make him tell.

Put, put, put, put. Shaniqua's father turned into the driveway on his motorcycle. The older girl veered along the path, tapping her cane on the bricks.

It had been a perfect 10th birthday.

No, a perfect *year.* Most dramatic of all had been his adventure on the Stagecoach Run. He'd gone to school with his elbow wrapped for a week.

"Bye, Whistling Boy!" Shaniqua yelled as the motorcycle zoomed away down his street.

Jake felt for his doorknob and stepped inside. He nabbed a lemon drop from the table in the entryway. Rowling, Squirt dug his claws into his shoulder to hold on. Jake slid into the kitchen on his socks. He had a sneaky suspicion there would be more Adventure Sports adventures in his life.

Many more...

About the Author

"More than anything else in the world," says Susan Clymer, "I love to write. There are other activities I enjoy…like wearing silly socks, observing animals and taking long wilderness hikes."

Ms. Clymer has written thirteen books for young readers, including *Llama Pajamas*, *Nine Lives of AdventureCat*, and *There's a Hamster in My Lunchbox*. A graduate of the University of California, Berkeley, Clymer leads rollicking professional development workshops for teachers and is a popular speaker at educational conferences. She often leads workshops at young authors' conferences. Ms. Clymer is committed to working with young people. Though she lives in the Midwest, she conducts one to four week Creative Writing residencies at schools across the United States and internationally.